A Ferrara wo... Baracchi tabl... ...ar or being poisoned.

So Fia had no idea why he was at her restaurant and terror rippled through her. He didn't know.

He couldn't know.

"Buena sera, Fia."

A deep male voice came from the doorway and she turned. Still the same "born to rule" Ferrara self-confidence; the same innate sophistication, polished until it shone bright as the paintwork of his Lamborghini. He was six foot three of hard, sensual masculinity, but Fia felt nothing a woman was supposed to feel when she laid eyes on Santino Ferrara.

He was her biggest mistake.

And judging from the cold, cynical glint in his eye, he considered her to be his.

Did he know?

Had he found out?

Fia wasn't fooled by his apparently relaxed pose or his deceptively mild tone.

Santino Ferrara was the most dangerous man she'd ever met.

All about the author...
Sarah Morgan

USA TODAY bestselling author **SARAH MORGAN** writes lively, sexy stories for both Harlequin Presents and Medical Romance.

As a child Sarah dreamed of being a writer and although she took a few interesting detours on the way, she is now living that dream. With her writing career she has successfully combined business with pleasure, and she firmly believes that reading romance is one of the most satisfying fat-free escapist pleasures available. Her stories are unashamedly optimistic and she is always pleased when she receives letters from readers saying that her books have helped them through hard times.

RT Book Reviews has described her writing as "action-packed and sexy" and nominated her books for their Reviewer's Choice Awards and their "Top Pick" slot.

Sarah lives near London with her husband and two children who innocently provide an endless supply of authentic dialogue. When she isn't writing or reading, Sarah enjoys music, movies and any activity that takes her outdoors.

Readers can find out more about Sarah and her books from her website, www.sarahmorgan.com. She can also be found on Facebook and Twitter.

Other titles by Sarah Morgan available in ebook

Harlequin Presents®

3043—ONCE A FERRARA WIFE...
  (linked to *The Forbidden Ferrara*)
3021—DOUKAKIS'S APPRENTICE
  (*21st Century Bosses*)
3000—A NIGHT OF SCANDAL
  (*The Notorious Wolfes*)

Sarah Morgan

THE FORBIDDEN FERRARA

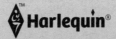

TORONTO NEW YORK LONDON
AMSTERDAM PARIS SYDNEY HAMBURG
STOCKHOLM ATHENS TOKYO MILAN MADRID
PRAGUE WARSAW BUDAPEST AUCKLAND

Recycling programs
for this product may
not exist in your area.

ISBN-13: 978-0-373-13074-0

THE FORBIDDEN FERRARA

Copyright © 2012 by Sarah Morgan

www.Harlequin.com

Printed in U.S.A.

THE FORBIDDEN FERRARA

For my editor Lucy Gilmour, who is wise, clever and always wears great shoes. Thank you.

CHAPTER ONE

THERE was a shocked silence round the boardroom table.

Amused by the reaction, Santo Ferrara sat back in his chair. 'I'm sure you'll all agree it's an exciting project,' he drawled. 'Thank you for your attention.'

'You've lost your mind.' It was his older brother who finally broke the silence. Cristiano, who had recently relinquished some of his responsibility in the company to spend more time with his young family. 'It can't be done.'

'Because you didn't succeed? Don't beat yourself up. It's fairly common for a man to lose his edge when he's distracted by a wife and kids.' Santo loaded his tone with sympathy, enjoying the brief interlude in what had been a long, punishing few weeks. And if he felt a slight twinge of envy that his brother had gone on to be as successful in his personal life as he was in business then he told himself that it was just a matter of time before he found the same thing himself. 'It's like seeing a great warrior fallen. Don't blame yourself. Living with three women can soften a man.'

The rest of the Board exchanged nervous glances but wisely chose to remain silent.

Cristiano's gaze locked on his. 'I am still chairman of this company.'

'Precisely. You've taken a back seat while you change nappies. Now leave the good ideas to the rest of us.' He was being deliberately combative and Cristiano gave a reluctant laugh.

'I'm not denying that your proposal is exciting. I can see the business potential in adapting the hotel to accommodate a wider range of sports and appeal to a younger demographic. I even agree that expanding on the West coast of Sicily has potential for a certain type of discerning traveller—' he paused and when he looked at Santo his eyes were deadly serious '—but the success of the project rests on you gaining the extra land from the Baracchi family and old man Baracchi would shoot you through the head before he sold to you.'

Good-natured banter gave way to tension. Those around the table kept their eyes down, everyone well aware of the history between the two families. The whole of Sicily knew the history.

'That is my problem to deal with,' Santo said in a cool tone and Cristiano made an impatient sound as he pushed back his chair and paced over to the expanse of glass that overlooked the glittering Mediterranean sea.

'Since you took over day-to-day running of the company you have more than proved yourself. You have done things I hadn't even thought of doing.' He turned. 'But you will not be able to do *this*. You will simply inflame a situation that has been simmering for almost three generations. You should let it die.'

'I am going to turn the Ferrara Beach Club into our most successful hotel.'

'You will fail.'

Santo smiled. 'Shall we bet on that?'

For once his brother didn't return the smile or take up the challenge. 'This goes deeper than sibling rivalry. You *cannot* do this.'

'Enough time has passed for us to put grievances aside.'

'That,' Cristiano said slowly, 'depends on the grievance.'

Santo felt the anger start to heat inside him but alongside the anger were darker, murkier emotions that sprang to life whenever the Baracchi name was mentioned. It was a visceral reaction, a conditioned response reinforced by a lifetime of animosity between the families. 'I was not responsible for what happened to Baracchi's grandson. You know the truth.'

'This is not about truth or reason, but about passion and prejudice. Deep-rooted prejudice. I have already approached him. Made him several more than generous offers. Baracchi would see his family starve before he sells his land to a Ferrara. Negotiations are closed.'

Santo rose to his feet. 'Then it's time they were reopened.'

A man cleared his throat. 'As your lawyer it's my duty to warn against—'

'Don't give me negatives—' Santo lifted his hand to silence the man, his eyes still fixed on his brother. 'So your objection isn't the commercial development which you concede makes sound business sense, but the interaction with the Baracchi family. Do you think I'm a coward?'

'No, and that is what troubles me. You use reason and courage but Baracchi has neither. You are my brother.' Cristiano's voice thickened. 'Guiseppe Baracchi hates you. He's always been an irascible old man. What makes you think he will listen to you before he loses that infamous temper of his?'

'He may be an irascible old man but he's also a frightened old man in financial trouble.'

'I'm willing to bet he's not in so much trouble he'll take money from a Ferrara. And frightened old men can be dangerous. We've maintained the hotel there because it would hurt our mother to sell our father's first hotel, but I've been talking to her recently and—'

'We're not going to sell. I'm going to turn it around but to do that I need the land. *All* of the land. The whole bay.' Santo saw the lawyer's agitation but he ignored him. 'I don't just want the land for watersports, I want the Beach Shack. That restaurant pulls in more custom than all our restaurants in the hotel. This is not about fuelling a feud, it's about protecting our business. While guests walk away from us to eat at the Beach Shack and watch the sunset, we are losing revenue.'

'Which brings us to the second problem in this ambitious scheme of yours. That restaurant is run by his granddaughter—a woman who very possibly hates you even more than her grandfather.' Cristiano looked him straight in the eye. 'How do you think Fia will greet the news that you intend to make an offer for the land?'

He didn't have to think. He knew.

She would fight him with everything she had.

They would clash. Tempers would burn hot.

And woven through the tension of the present would be the past.

Not just the long-standing feud over land, but their own personal history. Because he hadn't been entirely honest with his brother, had he? In a family where no one had secrets, he had a secret. A secret he'd buried deep enough to ensure it would never see the light of day.

The sudden rush of black emotion took him by surprise. With an impatient frown he glanced out of the window to the beach beyond but he didn't see sand or sea. Instead he saw Fiammetta Baracchi with her long legs and temper hotter than a red chilli pepper.

Cristiano was still watching him. 'She hates you.'

Was it hate?

They hadn't discussed feelings, he thought. They hadn't discussed anything at all. Not even when they'd ripped each other's clothes off, when his body had screamed for hers and hers for his, not once in the whole wild, erotic, out of control experience had they exchanged a single word.

And instinct told him she'd buried her secret as deeply as he'd buried his.

As far as he was concerned, that was the way it was staying.

The past had no place in this negotiation.

'Under her management the Shack has gone from a few rickety tables on the beach to the most talked about eatery in Sicily. Rumour has it that she's a talented chef.'

Cristiano shook his head slowly. 'You're walking into an explosive situation, Santo. At best it's going to be messy.'

Carlo, their lawyer, put his head in his hands.

Santo ignored both of them just as he ignored the elemental rush of heat and the dark memories that, now woken, refused to return to sleep. 'This feud has lasted too long. It's time to move on.'

'Not possible.' Cristiano's voice was harsh. 'Guiseppe Baracchi's grandson, his only male heir, died when he wrapped a car around a tree. *Your* car, Santo. And you expect him to shake your hand and sell you his land?'

'Guiseppe Baracchi is a businessman and this deal makes perfect business sense.'

'Are you going to tell him that before or after the old man shoots you?'

'He won't shoot me.'

'He probably won't need to.' Cristiano gave a grim smile. 'Knowing Fia, she'll shoot you first.'

And that, Santo thought without emotion, *was entirely possible.*

'This is the last snapper.' Fia lifted the fish from the grill and plated it up. The heat from the fire warmed her cheeks. 'Gina?'

'Gina is outside checking out the driver of a Lamborghini that just pulled into our car park. You know she has a taste for men who can keep her in the style of her dreams. I'll take those.' Ben scooped up the plates and balanced them. 'How is your grandfather tonight?'

'Tired. He's not himself. He doesn't even have the energy to snap at people.' Fia felt a ripple of worry and made a mental note to check on him next time she had a lull. 'Are you coping out there? Tell Gina to leave the customers alone and work.'

'You tell her. I'm too chicken.' Ben skilfully dodged the waitress, who came sprinting into the kitchen. 'Hey, be careful or we'll be sending you out on the boat for more snapper.'

'You'll *never* guess who just turned up—'

Fia shot a glance at Ben as she started on the next order. 'Serve the food or it will be cold and I don't serve cold food.' Aware that Gina was virtually trembling with excitement, Fia decided it would be quicker and more efficient just to let her gush. She added seasoning and olive oil to fresh scallops and dropped them onto the pan. They were so fresh they needed nothing but the best quality oil to bring out the flavour. 'It must be someone exciting because I've never known you starstruck before and we've had plenty of celebrities in here.' As far as she was concerned, a guest was a guest. They were here to eat and her job was to feed them. And she fed them well. Expertly she flipped the scallops and added fresh herbs and capers to the pan.

Gina sneaked a look over her shoulder to the restaurant. 'It's the first time I've seen him in person. He's stunning.'

'Whoever he is, I hope he booked because otherwise you're going to have to send him away.' Fia shook the pan constantly. 'It's a full house tonight.'

'You won't be sending him away.' Gina sounded awestruck. 'It's Santo Ferrara. In the flesh. Only sadly not showing anywhere near as much flesh as I'd like in an ideal world.'

Fia stopped breathing.

Weakness spread through her body and then she started to shake, as if she'd suddenly been injected with something deadly. The pan slid from her hand and crashed onto the flame, the precious scallops forgotten.

'He wouldn't come here.' *He wouldn't dare.* She was talking to herself. Reassuring herself. But there was no reassurance to be had.

Since when did she know anything about what motivated Santo Ferrara?

'Er—why wouldn't he come?' Gina looked intrigued. 'Seems logical enough to me. His company owns the hotel next door and you serve great food.'

Gina wasn't local, otherwise she would have known the history between the two families. Everyone knew. And Fia also knew that the Ferrara Beach Club, the hotel that shared her perfect curve of beach, was the smallest and least significant of the Ferrara hotel group. There was no earthly reason why Santo himself would choose to give it his personal attention.

Her concentration shot, Fia caught her elbow on the side of a hot pan. Pain seared through her and brought her back to the present. Furious with herself for forgetting the scallops, she plated them up with meticulous care and handed them to Gina, functioning on automatic. 'This is for the couple on the waterfront,' she croaked. 'It's their anniversary and they booked this six months ago so make sure you treat them with reverence. This is a big night for them. I don't want them disappointed.'

Gina gaped at her. 'Aren't you going to—'

'I'm fine! It's just burned flesh—' Fia spoke through her teeth '—I'll put it under cold water in a minute.'

'I wasn't thinking about your elbow. I was thinking about the fact that Santo Ferrara is standing in your restaurant and you don't seem to care,' Gina said faintly. 'You treat every customer like royalty and when someone genuinely important turns up you ignore him. You do know who he is? *The* Ferrara, yes? Ferrara Resorts. Five star all the way.'

'I know exactly who he is.'

'But Boss, if he's come here to eat—'

'He hasn't come here to eat.' A Ferrara would never sit down at a Baracchi table for fear of being poisoned. She had no idea why he was here and that lack of insight frustrated her because she couldn't fight what she didn't understand. And mingled in with the shock and anger was dread.

He'd walked boldly into her restaurant at peak time. Why?

Only something really, really important would make him do that.

Terror rippled through her. *No*, she thought wildly, *it couldn't possibly be that.*

He didn't know.

He *couldn't* know.

With a final curious glance, Gina hurried out of the kitchen and Fia ran cold water over her burned elbow, trying to reassure herself that it was a routine visit. Another attempt by the Ferrara family to hold out an olive branch. There had been others, and her grandfather had taken each and every olive branch and snapped it in two. Since her brother's death, there had been nothing. No overtures. No contact.

Until now…

Functioning on automatic, she reached above her head for a fresh bulb of garlic. She grew it herself in her garden, along with vegetables and herbs and she enjoyed the growing almost as much as she enjoyed the cooking. It soothed her. Gave her a feeling of home and family she'd never derived from the people around her. Reaching for her favourite knife, she started chopping, trying to think how she would have reacted if the circumstances had been different. If the terror wasn't involved. If the stakes weren't so high—

She would have been cold. Businesslike.

'*Buonasera*, Fia.'

A deep male voice came from the doorway and she turned, the knife turning from a kitchen implement to a weapon. The crazy thing was, she didn't know his voice. But she knew his eyes and they were looking at her now—two dark pools of dangerous black. They gleamed bright with intelligence and hard with ruthless purpose. They were the eyes of a man who thrived in a cut-throat business environment. A man who knew what he wanted and wasn't afraid to go after it. They were the same eyes that had glittered into hers in the darkness three years before as they'd ripped each other's clothes and slaked a fierce hunger.

Those three years had added a couple of inches to his broad shoulders and more bulk to muscles she remembered all too well. Apart from that he was exactly the same. Still the same 'born to rule' Ferrara self-confidence; the same innate sophistication, polished until it shone bright as the paintwork of his Lamborghini. He was six foot three of hard, sensual masculinity but Fia felt nothing a woman was supposed to feel when she laid eyes on Santo Ferrara. A normal woman wouldn't feel this searing anger, this almost uncontrollable urge to scratch his handsome face and thump that powerful chest. When she was near him, every feeling was exaggerated. She felt vulnerable and defenceless and those feelings brought out the worst in her. Usually she was warm and civil to everyone who stepped inside her kitchen. Reviews commended her hospitality and the intimate, friendly atmosphere of the restaurant. But she couldn't even bring herself to wish this man a good evening. And that was because she didn't want him to have a good evening.

She wanted him to go to hell and stay there.

He was her biggest mistake.

And judging from the cold, cynical glint in his eye, he considered her to be his.

'Well, this is a surprise. The Ferrara brothers don't usually step down from their ivory tower to mingle with us mortals. Checking out the competition?' She adopted her most businesslike tone, while all the time her anxiety was rising and the questions were pounding through her head.

Did he know?

Had he found out?

A faint smile touched his mouth and the movement distracted her. There was an almost deadly beauty in the sensual curve of those lips. Everything about the man was dark and sexual, as if he'd been designed for the express purpose of drawing women to their doom. If rumour were correct, he did that with appalling frequency.

Fia wasn't fooled by his apparently relaxed pose or his deceptively mild tone.

Santo Ferrara was the most dangerous man she'd ever met.

Without exchanging words, she'd fallen. Even now, years later, she didn't understand what had happened that night. One moment she'd been alone with her misery. The next, his hand had been on her shoulder and everything that had happened after that was a blur. Had it been about human comfort? Possibly, except that comfort implied gentle emotions and those had been in short supply that night.

He watched her now, his face giving no hint as to his thoughts. 'I've heard good things about your restaurant. I've come to find out if any of them are true.'

He didn't know, she thought. *If he knew, he wouldn't be toying with her.*

'They're all true, but I'm afraid I can't satisfy your curiosity. We're fully booked.' Her lips formed the words while her mind raced over the possible reasons for his visit. Was that really all this was? An idle visit to check out the competition? No, surely not. Santo Ferrara would delegate that task to a minion. Her brain throbbed with the strain of trying to second-guess him.

'We both know you can find me a table if you want to.'

'But I don't want to.' Her fingers tightened on the knife. 'Since when did a Ferrara dine at the same table as a Baracchi?'

His eyes locked on hers. Her heart beat just a little bit faster.

The searing look he sent her from under those dense, inky lashes reminded her that once they hadn't just dined; they'd hungered and they'd feasted. They'd devoured each other and taken until there was nothing left to take. And she could still remember the taste of him; feel the rippling power of his body against hers as they'd indulged in dark, forbidden pleasure, the memory of which had never left her.

In a crowded room she wouldn't have known his voice, but she knew how he'd feel and her palms grew hot and her knees weakened as her thoughts broke free of the restraints she'd imposed, liberating memories so vivid that for a moment she couldn't breathe.

He smiled.

Not the smile of a friend, but the smile of a conqueror contemplating the imminent surrender of a captive. 'Eat at my table, Fia.'

His casual use of her name suggested a familiarity that didn't exist and it unbalanced her, as he'd no doubt intended. He was a man who always had to be in control. He'd been in control on that night and there had been something terrifying about the force of passion he'd unleashed.

She'd taken him because she'd been in desperate need of human comfort.

He'd taken her because he could.

'This is *my* table we're talking about,' she said in a clear voice, 'and you're not invited.' She had to get rid of him. The longer he stayed, the bigger the risk to her. 'You have your own restaurant next door. If you're hungry then I'm sure they'd accommodate you, although I admit that neither the food nor the view is as good as mine so I can understand why you find both lacking.'

There was a stillness about him that made her uneasy. A watchfulness that she didn't trust.

'I need to speak to your grandfather. Tell me where he is.'

So that was why he was here. Another round of fruitless negotiations that would lead the same way as the others. Thanks goodness he'd made this visit at night, she thought numbly. No matter what happened, she had to ensure he didn't return during the day. 'You must have a death wish. You know how he feels about you.'

Those eyes were hooded as he watched her. 'And does he know how *you* feel about me?'

His oblique reference to that night shocked her because it was something that had never been mentioned before.

Was he threatening her? Was he about to expose her?

Relief had been replaced by sick panic as various avenues of horror opened up before her. Was that why he'd done it? To have a hold over her in the future? 'My grandfather is old and unwell. If you have something to say you can say it to me. If you want to talk business, then you'll talk to me. I run the restaurant.'

'But the land is his.' His soft voice was a million times more disturbing than an explosion of temper and that control of his worried her because she felt none where he was concerned. She thought about what she'd read—about Santo Ferrara more than filling his brother's large shoes in his running of their global corporation. And suddenly she realised how foolish she'd been to think that the Beach Club was too insignificant to be of interest to the big boss. It was precisely *because* it was too insignificant that it had caught his attention. He wanted to expand the Beach Club, and to do that he needed—

'You want our land?'

'It was once *our* land,' he said with lethal emphasis, 'until one of your unscrupulous relatives, of which there have been all too many, chose to use blackmail to extract half the beach from my great-grandfather. Unlike him, I am willing to propose a fair deal and pay you a generous price to regain that which should never have left my family.'

And it was all about money, of course. The Ferraras thought everything could be bought.

Which was what frightened her.

The initial feeling of relief that had flooded her had been replaced by trepidation. If he were intent on developing the land then she'd never be safe.

'My grandfather will never, ever sell to you so if that is what this visit is about you're wasting your time. You might as well go back to New York or Rome or wherever it is you live these days. Pick another project.'

'I live here.' His lip curled. 'And I am giving this project my personal attention.'

It was the worst news she could have had. 'He hasn't been well. I won't let you upset him.'

'Your grandfather is tough as boots. I doubt he is in need of your protection.' A few layers of 'civilized' had melted away and the dangerous edge to his tone told her that he meant business. 'Does he know that you're deliberately attracting my customers away from the hotel to your restaurant?'

He was six foot three of prime masculinity, the force of his nature barely leashed beneath that outward appearance of sophistication. And Fia knew just how much heat bubbled under the cool surface. She'd been burned by that heat.

His passion has shocked her, but nowhere near as much as her own.

'If by "deliberately" you mean that I'm cooking them good food in great surroundings, then I'm guilty as charged.'

'Those "great surroundings" are exactly the reason I'm here.'

So that was what had brought him back. Not the night they'd shared. Not concern for her welfare or anything that was personal.

Just business.

If she weren't so relieved that there wasn't a deeper reason, she would have been appalled by his insensitivity. Whatever else had happened, a death lay between them. Blood had been shed.

But one inconvenient death wouldn't be enough to stand in the way of a Ferrara on the path to acquisition, she thought numbly. It was all about empire building. 'This conversation is over. I need to cook. I'm in the middle of service.' The truth was she'd all but finished, but she'd wanted him out of here.

But of course he didn't leave because a Ferrara only ever did what a Ferrara wanted to do.

Instead of walking away he lounged against the door frame, sleek and confident, those eyes fixed on her. 'You feel so threatened by me you have to have a knife in your hand while we talk?'

'I'm not threatened. I'm working.'

'I could disarm you in under five seconds.'

'I could cut you to the bone in less.' It was bravado, of course, because not for one moment did she underestimate his strength.

'If this is the welcome you give your customers I'm surprised you have anyone here at all. Not exactly warm, is it?' The fringe of thick lashes made his eyes seem darker. Or maybe the darkness was something they created together.

She knew that the addition of just one ingredient could alter flavour. In this case it was the forbidden. They'd done the unforgivable. The unexplainable. The inexcusable.

'You're not a customer, Santo.'

'So feed me and then I will be. Cook me dinner.'

Cook me dinner. Just for a moment her hands shook.

He'd walked away without once glancing back. That, she could handle because, apart from one night of reckless sex, they'd shared nothing. The fact that he'd played a much bigger role in her dreams wasn't his fault. But for him to walk back in here and order her to cook him dinner, as if his return was something to celebrate...

The audacity of it took her breath away. 'Sorry. Fatted calf isn't on the menu tonight. Now get the hell out of my kitchen, Santo. Gina manages the bookings and tonight we're full. And tomorrow night. And any other night you wish to eat in my restaurant.'

'Gina is the pretty blonde? I noticed her on the way in.'

Of course he would have noticed her. Santo Ferrara not noticing a blonde, curvy woman would be like a lion not noticing a cute impala. That didn't surprise her. What surprised her was the ache in her chest. She didn't want to care who this man took to his bed. She'd never wanted to care and the fact that she did terrified her more than anything. She'd grown up witnessing that caring meant pain.

Never love a Sicilian man had been the last words her mother had flung at her eight-year-old daughter before she'd walked out of the door for ever.

Afraid of her own feelings, Fia turned her back and finished chopping garlic, but they were the ragged, uneven cuts of an amateur, not a professional.

'It's dangerous to handle a knife when your hands are shaking.' Suddenly he was right behind her, too close for comfort, and she felt her pulse sprint because even though he wasn't touching her she could feel the warmth of him, the power of him and feel her answering response. It was immediate and visceral and she almost screamed with frustration because it made no sense. It was like salivating over a food that she knew would make her ill.

'I'm not shaking.'

'No?' A strong, bronzed hand covered hers and immediately she was back in the darkness of that night, his mouth burning against hers, his skilled fingers showing her no mercy as he drove her wild. 'Do you think about it?'

She didn't need to ask what he meant.

Did she think about it? Oh, God, he had no idea. She'd tried everything, *everything*, to wipe the memory of that night from her mind but it was always with her. A sensual scar that was never going to heal. 'Take your hand off mine right now.'

His hand tightened, the strength in those fingers holding hers still. 'You finish serving food at ten. We'll talk after that.'

It was a command not an invitation and the sure confidence with which he issued that command licked at the flames of her anger. 'My work doesn't finish when the restaurant closes. I have hours of work and when that is done I go to bed.'

'With that puppy-eyed boy who works for you? Playing it safe now, Fia?'

She was so shocked by the question that she turned her head to look at him and the movement brought her physically closer. The light brush of her skin against the hardness of his thigh triggered a frightening response. It was as if her body *knew*. 'Who I invite into my bed is none of your business.'

Their eyes met briefly as they acknowledged privately what they'd never acknowledged publicly.

She watched, transfixed, as his gaze turned black.

A long dormant feeling slowly uncurled itself inside her, a response she didn't want to feel for this man.

What might have happened next she'd never know because Gina walked in and when Fia saw who she was carrying she wanted to shout out a warning. She wanted to tell the other girl to run and not look back. But it was too late. Her luck had run out. It was over. It was over because Santo was already turning to locate the source of the interruption, an irritated frown scoring the bronzed planes of his handsome face.

'He had a bad dream—' Gina cooed, stroking the sobbing toddler. 'I said I'd bring him to his mamma as you've finished cooking for the night.'

Fia stood, powerless to do anything except allow events to unfold.

Had circumstances been different she would have been pleased to see a Ferrara shocked out of his customary cool. As it was the stakes were so high she watched with the breath trapped in her lungs, reluctant witness to his rapidly changing emotions.

His initial irritation at the disturbance gave way to puzzlement as he looked at the miserable, hiccuping child now stretching out his little arms to Fia.

And she took him, of course, because his welfare mattered to her above all other things.

And two things happened.

Her son stared curiously at the tall, dark stranger in the kitchen and stopped crying instantly.

And the tall, dark stranger stared into black eyes almost identical to his own, and turned pale as death.

CHAPTER TWO

'CRISTO—' His voice hoarse, Santo took a step backwards and crashed into some pans that had been neatly stacked ready to be put away. Startled by the sudden noise, the child flinched and hid his face in his mother's neck. Aware that he was the cause of that sudden display of anxiety, Santo struggled for control. Only by the most ruthless application of willpower did he succeed in hauling back the searing anger that threatened to erupt.

From the security of his mother's arms, the child peeped at him in terror, instinctively hiding from danger and yet intrigued by it.

And she would have been hiding, too, Santo thought grimly, if she had anywhere to hide. But she was right out in the open, all her secrets exposed.

He didn't even need to ask the obvious question.

Even without that instant moment of recognition he would have seen it in the way she held herself. That raw, undiluted anxiety was visible to the naked eye.

He'd come here to negotiate the purchase of the land. Not for one second had he anticipated *this*.

From the moment he'd walked into the kitchen she'd been in a hurry to get rid of him, and now he understood why. He'd assumed their past history was to blame for her response. And of course it was. But not in the way he'd thought.

There was a heaviness in his chest, as if his heart were being squeezed in a clenched fist.

Confronted by a situation he hadn't anticipated, he struggled with emotions that were new to him. Not just anger but a deep, primitive desire to protect.

The weight in his chest bloomed and grew into something so huge and powerful he felt the force of it right through his body.

I'm a father.

But even as he thought it, he also thought, *this is not how it was supposed to be.*

He'd always assumed that he would eventually fall in love, marry and then have children. He was a traditional guy, wasn't he? He'd seen his brother's joy and his sister's joy and he'd arrogantly assumed that the same experience awaited him.

He'd missed it all, he thought bitterly. The birth, first steps, first words—

Tormented by those thoughts, Santo gave a low growl.

The toddler's eyes widened with alarm as he sensed the change in the atmosphere. Or perhaps it was just that he detected his mother's panic. Either way, Santo knew enough about children to know that this one was about to dissolve into screams.

With another huge effort of will, he forced himself to suppress his feelings. It was the hardest thing he'd ever done. 'It is late for someone so young to be up.' He injected his voice with the right amount of gentleness, focusing on the child rather than the mother. Even looking at the boy sent a searing pain through his chest. It was a physical effort not to grab him, strap him into the seat of his Lamborghini and drive away with him. 'You must be very tired, *chicco*. You should be in bed.'

Fia stiffened, clearly taking that as criticism. 'He has bad dreams sometimes.'

The news that his son suffered from bad dreams did nothing to improve Santo's black, dangerous mood. What, he wondered darkly, had caused those dreams? Reminded of just how dysfunctional this family was, anger turned to cold dread.

'Gina—is it Gina?' He glanced at the pretty waitress and somehow managed to deliver the smile that had never failed him yet and it didn't fail him now as the girl beamed at him, visibly overwhelmed by his status.

'Signor Ferrara—'

'I really need to speak to Fia in private—'

'No!' Fia's voice bordered on desperate. 'Not now. Can't you see that this is a really bad time?'

'Oh, it's fine,' Gina gushed helpfully, blushing under Santo's warm, approving gaze. 'I can take him. I'm his nanny.'

'Nanny?' The word stuck in Santo's throat. No one in his family had ever employed outside help to care for their children. 'You look after him?' He didn't trust himself to use the words 'my son'. Not yet.

'It's a team approach,' Gina said cheerfully. 'We're like meerkats. We all look after the young. Only in this case there is only one young so he's horribly spoiled. I look after him when Fia is working, but I knew she'd finished cooking tonight so I thought I'd bring him for a cuddle. Now he's calmed down he's going to be just fine. He'll go straight off again the moment I put him in his bed. Come to Auntie Gina—' Cooing at the sleepy child, she drew him out of Fia's reluctant arms and snuggled him close.

'We still have customers—'

'They're virtually all finished,' Gina said helpfully. 'Just waiting for table two to pay the bill. Ben has it all under control. You have your chat, Boss.' Apparently oblivious to the tension crackling around them, Gina cast a final awestruck glance at Santo and melted from the room.

Silence reigned.

Fia stood, her cheeks pale against the fire of her hair, dark smudges under her eyes.

Words were some of the most deadly tools in his armoury. He used them to negotiate impossible deals, to smooth the most difficult of situations, to hire and fire, but suddenly, when he needed them more than ever before, they were absent. All he managed was a single word.

'Well?'

Despite his heightened emotional state, or perhaps because of it, Santo spoke softly but she flinched as if he'd raised his voice.

'Well, what?'

'Don't even think about giving me anything other than the truth. You'd be wasting your breath.'

'In that case why ask?'

He didn't know what to say to her. She didn't know what to say to him.

Their situation was painfully difficult.

Before tonight they'd never actually spoken. Even during that one turbulent encounter, they hadn't spoken. Not one word had been exchanged. Oh, there'd been sounds. The ripping of clothes, the slide of flesh against flesh, ragged breathing—but no words. Nothing coherent from either of them. He was a man confident in his sexuality, but he still didn't really understand what had happened that night.

Had the whole forbidden nature of their encounter acted as some sort of powerful aphrodisiac? Had the fact that their two families had been enemies for almost three generations added to the emotion that had brought them together like animals in the darkness?

Possibly. Either way, their relationship had been like a blast from a rocket engine, the sudden heat tearing through both of them, burning up common sense and reason. He should have known there would be a price. And clearly he'd been paying that price for the last three years.

'Why the hell didn't you tell me?' His tone was raw and ragged and he watched as her breathing grew shallow.

'For a supposedly clever man you ask stupid questions.'

'Nothing—*nothing*—that has happened between our two families should have prevented you from telling me *this*.' With a slice of his hand he gestured towards the open door. 'This' had vanished into the night with the accommodating Gina and letting him out of his sight was one of the hardest things Santo had ever done. Soon, he vowed. Soon, the child would never be out of his sight again. It was the only sure thing in this storm of uncertainty. 'You should have told me.'

'For what purpose? To have my son exposed to the same bitter feud that has coloured our entire lives? To have him used as some pawn in your power games? I have protected him from all of that.'

'*Our* son—' Santo spoke in a thickened tone '—he is my son, too. The product of both of us.'

'He is the product of one night when you and I were—'

'—were what?'

Her gaze didn't falter. 'We were foolish. Out of control. We did something stupid. Something we *never* should have done. I don't want to talk about it.'

'Well, tough, because you're going to talk about it. You should have talked about it three years ago when you first realised you were pregnant.'

'Oh, don't be so naive!' Her temper flared as hot as his. 'This was not some cosy romance that had unexpected consequences. It was complicated.'

'The decision whether or not to tell a man he's the father of your child is not complicated. *Cristo*—' Floored by the monumental issues facing them, he let out a long breath and dragged his hand over the back of his neck, seeking calm and not finding it anywhere within his grasp. 'I cannot believe this. I need time to think.' He knew that decisions made in the heat of anger were never good ones and he needed them to be good ones.

'There is nothing to think about.'

Santo cast his mind back to that night, a night he never allowed himself to think about because the good was irrevocably entwined with the really, really bad and it was impossible to unravel the two. 'How did it happen? I used—'

'Apparently there are some things even a Ferrara can't control,' she said coolly, 'and this was one of them.'

He looked at her blankly. The whole night had merged for him. Pulling out details was impossible. It had been crazy, wild and—she was right—ill-advised. But what they'd shared hadn't been the product of rational decision-making. It had been sheer animal lust, the like of which he'd never experienced before or since.

She'd been upset.

He'd put his hand on her shoulder.

She'd turned to him.

And that had been it—

Such a small spark to light such a raging fire.

And then, even before the heat had cooled, she'd had the call telling her that her brother had been killed. That single tragic phone call that had sliced through their loving like the blade of a guillotine. And after, the fallout. The recriminations and the speculation.

The young waiter appeared in the doorway, his eyes on Fia. 'Is everything OK? I saw Luca awake, which is always nice because I managed to snatch a lovely cuddle, but I heard raised voices.' He shot Santo a suspicious look, which Santo returned tenfold. The news that everyone appeared to be cuddling his son except him simply fuelled his already fiercely burning temper. An unfamiliar emotion streaked through him—the primal response of a man guarding his territory.

So his child was called Luca.

The fact that he'd learned the name from this man drove him to the edge of control.

What exactly was his relationship with Fia?

'This is a private conversation. Get out,' he said thickly and he heard Fia's soft intake of breath.

'It's OK, Ben. Just go.'

Apparently Ben didn't know what was good for him because he stood stubbornly in the doorway. 'I'm not leaving until I know you're all right.' It was like a spaniel challenging a Rottweiler. He glared at Santo, who would have given him points for courage had he not been way past admiring the qualities of another man. Especially a man who was making puppy eyes at the woman who, only moments earlier, had been clutching his child.

'I am giving you one more opportunity to leave and then I will remove you myself.'

'Go, Ben!' She sounded exasperated. 'You're just giving him another reason to throw his weight around.'

Ben gave her one last doubtful look and melted away into the darkness of the night, leaving the two of them alone.

Tension throbbed like a living force. The air was heavy with it. He could taste it on his tongue and feel the weight of it pressing down on his shoulders. And he knew she could feel it too.

His head was a mass of questions.

How had no one guessed? Had no one questioned the identity of the child's father? He didn't understand how she could have hidden such a thing.

'You knew you were pregnant and yet you cut me out of your life.'

'You were never in my life, Santo. And I was never in yours.'

'We made a child together.' His low growl came from somewhere deep inside him and he saw her recoil as if the reminder came as a physical blow.

'You need to calm down. In just ten minutes you've frightened my child, virtually seduced his nanny, bawled me out and been unforgivably rude to someone I care about.'

'I did *not* frighten our child.' That accusation angered him more than any of the others. 'You did that by creating this situation.' And he still didn't understand how she had kept her secret. His usually sharp mind refused to work. 'This is your grandfather's idea of revenge? Punishing the Ferraras by hiding the child?'

'No!' Her chest rose and fell, her breathing shallow. 'He adores Luca.'

Santo raised his eyebrows in disbelief. 'He adores a child who is half Ferrara? You expect me to believe that age has finally gifted a Baracchi with tolerance?' He broke off, alerted by something in her eyes, some instinct that went bone-deep. And suddenly it fell into place. Finally he understood the truth and the reality was another blow to his already aching gut. '*Cristo*, he doesn't know, does he?' It was the only possible explanation and one that was confirmed by the look in her eyes.

'Santo—'

'Answer me.' His voice didn't sound like his own and he saw her take a step backwards. 'You *will* tell me the truth. He doesn't know, does he? You haven't told him.'

'How could I tell him?' Underneath the desperation was a profound weariness, as if this issue were a heavy weight she'd been carrying for too long. 'He hates everything about your family, and he hates *you* more than any man on the planet. Not just because your surname is Ferrara, but because—' She didn't finish the sentence and he let it hang there because to get involved in a discussion about her brother's death would mean being sidetracked, and he refused to be sidetracked.

They had a child.

A child that was half Ferrara, half Baracchi. An unimaginable bloodline.

A child born out of one night that had ended in tragedy.

And the old man didn't know.

He wondered how her grandfather could not have seen what he himself had seen instantly.

White-faced, she stared at him. Santo was so shell-shocked by the enormity of the secret she'd been carrying, he was reeling from it. How had she done it? She must have lain there every morning wondering whether today would be the day she'd be found out. Whether today would be the day a Ferrara would come and claim their own.

'*Madre de Dio*, I cannot believe this. When the child is old enough to ask about his father, what did you intend to tell him? On second thought, don't answer that,' he said thickly, 'I am not ready to hear the answer.' He knew as well as anyone that life was no fairy story, but belief in the sanctity of family ran strong in his veins. Family was the raft that kept you afloat in stormy seas, the anchor that stopped you from drifting, the wind in the sail that propelled you forward. He was the product of his parents' happy marriage and both his brother and sister had found love and created their own families. He'd assumed that the same would happen to him. Not once had he considered that he would have to fight for the right to be a father to his own child. Nor had he dreamt of his child being raised in a family like the Baracchis. He wouldn't have wished it on anyone. It was a nightmare almost too painful to contemplate.

Her breathing was shallow. 'Please, you have to promise me that you will let me deal with this. My grandfather is old.

He isn't well.' Her voice shook but Santo felt no sympathy. He felt bitter and angry and *raw*.

'You have had three years to deal with it. Now it's my turn. Did you really think I'd allow my son to be raised in your family? And without a father in his life? The notion of family is alien to a Baracchi.' He jabbed his fingers into his hair, his stress levels turning supersonic. 'When I think what the child must have gone through—'

'Luca is happy and well cared for.'

'I saw your childhood.' Santo let his hand fall to his side. 'I saw how it was for you. You don't understand what a family should be.' And it broke his heart that his son had been raised in a family like that.

Her face was ghostly pale. 'Luca's childhood is nothing like mine. And if you know what mine was like then you should also know that I would never want that for my son. I don't blame you for your concern but you are wrong. I *do* understand what a family should be. I always have.'

'How? Where would you learn that? Certainly not in your own home.' Her home life had been fractured, messy and unbelievably insecure because the Baracchi family didn't just fight their neighbours, they fought amongst themselves. If family was a boat built to weather stormy seas, then hers was a shipwreck.

The first time they'd met properly she'd been eight years old and hiding on the far side of the beach. *His* side, where no Baracchi was supposed to tread. She'd taken refuge in the disused boathouse, amongst jagged planks of wood and the acrid smell of oil. He'd been fourteen years old and totally at a loss to know what to do with his wild-haired intruder. Was he supposed to hold her captive? Ask for a ransom? In the end he'd done neither. Nor had he blown her cover.

Instead, intrigued by her defiance, spurred on by the lure

of the forbidden, he'd let her hide there until she'd chosen to return home.

Weeks later he'd found out that the day she'd kept her solitary vigil in his boathouse had been the day her mother had walked out, leaving Fia's violent Sicilian father to cope with two children he'd never wanted. He remembered being surprised that she hadn't cried. It was years before he realised that Fia never cried. She kept all her emotions hidden inside and never expected comfort. Which was probably because she'd learned there was none to be had in her family.

Santo's mouth tightened.

Maybe she did shut people out, but there was no way in hell he'd let her shut him out. Not now. Not this time. 'You made your decision, by yourself with no reference to anyone else. Now I will make mine.' He cut her no slack. Didn't allow the beseeching look in her eyes to alter him from what he knew to be the right course of action.

'What do you mean?'

'When I'm ready to talk, I'll contact you. And don't even *think* of running because if you do I will hunt you down. There is nowhere you can hide. Nowhere on this planet you can take my son that I can't find you.'

'He is my son, too.'

Santo gave a humourless smile. 'And that presents us with an interesting challenge, doesn't it? He is possibly the first thing our two families have had in common. When I've decided what I'm going to do about that, I'll let you know.'

As the furious growl of the Lamborghini disturbed the silence of the night, Fia just made it to the bathroom and was violently sick. It could have been panic, fear, or some noxious combination of the two, but whatever it was it left her shaking and she hated the weakness and the feeling of vulnerability. Afterwards she sat on the floor with her eyes closed, trying to formulate a plan but there was no plan she could make that he couldn't sweep aside.

He would take control, the way the Ferraras always took control. His contempt for her family would drive his decision-making. And part of her didn't blame him for that. In his position she probably would have felt the same way because, now, she understood how it felt to want to protect a child.

Fia wrapped her arms around her knees and pulled them closer, tucking herself into as small a space as possible.

He hadn't listened when she'd tried to explain herself. He hadn't believed her when she'd told him that she'd made sure that Luca's childhood was nothing like her own.

His mission now was to rescue his son from the Baracchi family.

There would be no softness. No concessions. No compromise.

Instead of being raised in a calm, loving atmosphere, Luca would be subjected to the intolerable pressures of animosity and resentment. He'd be the rope in an emotional tug of war.

And that was precisely why she'd chosen this particular rocky, deadly path and she'd lived with the lies, the worry and the stress for three years in order to protect her son.

'Mamma sick.' Luca stood there, his favourite bear clutched in his arms, that dark hair rumpled. The harsh bathroom lights spotlighted every feature and for a moment she couldn't breathe because right there, in her son's face, she saw Santo. Their child had inherited those unforgettable eyes, that same glossy dark hair. Even the shape of his mouth reminded her of his father and she wasn't going to start thinking about his stubborn streak…

Realistically, it had only been a matter of time before her secret was out.

'I love you.' Impulsively she dragged him into her arms and kissed his head, letting the warmth of him flow into her.

'I'm always going to be here for you. And Gina, and Ben. You have people who love you. You won't ever be alone.' She held him tightly, as she had never been held. She kissed him, as she had never been kissed. Perhaps it wasn't fair to blame Santo Ferrara for assuming that his child was being raised in a toxic atmosphere. He had no idea how hard she'd worked to ensure that Luca's childhood was nothing like her own.

And as he snuggled against her, happy and content, she felt her eyes fill.

What had she lacked, she wondered, that her own mother hadn't felt this same powerful bond? Nothing, *nothing*, would induce her to walk away from her child. There was no price, no power, no promise that could make her do such a thing.

And there was no way she was going to let Santo take her son.

Blissfully ignorant of the fact that their lives were teetering on the edge of a dangerous chasm, he wriggled out of her arms.

'Bed.'

'Good idea,' she croaked, scooping him up and carrying him back to his bed. Whatever happened, she was going to protect him from the fallout of this. She wasn't going to let him be hurt.

'Man come back?'

Her insides churned again. 'Yes, he'll come back.' She was in no doubt about that. And when he returned he'd bring serious legal muscle. She had no doubt about that, either. Events had been set in motion and there was no stopping them. No stopping a Ferrara from getting what he wanted.

And Santo Ferrara wanted his son.

She sat on the bed, watching her son fall asleep, her love for him so huge that it filled every part of her. The strength of that bond made it all too easy for her to imagine Santo's feelings. Deep inside her, the guilt that she worked so hard to suppress awoke.

She'd never been comfortable with her decision. It had haunted her in the dark hours of the night when there were no distractions to occupy her mind. It wasn't that she regretted the choice she'd made. She didn't. But she'd learned that the right decision could feel completely wrong. And then there were the dreams. Dreams that distorted reality. Twisted the impossible into the possible. Dreams of a life that didn't exist.

Blocking out images of black, silky lashes and a hard, sensual mouth, Fia stayed until Luca was safely asleep and then returned to the kitchen to clear up. Because she'd sent the staff home she had to do it herself, but the mindless work helped calm the panicky knot in her stomach. She poured her anxiety into each swipe of her cloth until every surface in the kitchen shone, until sweat pricked her brow, until she was too bone-tired to feel anything except the physical ache of hard labour. And then she grabbed a cold beer from the fridge and took it to the small wooden jetty that butted out from the restaurant.

Fishing boats bobbed quietly in the darkness, waiting to be taken out onto the water.

Usually this was a time to be calm, but tonight her nightly ritual failed to produce the desired effect.

Fia kicked off her shoes and sat on the jetty, feet dangling in the cool water, her gaze sliding to the lights of the Ferrara Beach Club on the opposite side of the bay. Eighty per cent of her customers tonight had come from the hotel. She had reservations for plenty more, booked months ahead. Twisting off the cap, she lifted the bottle to her lips, realising that by being good at what she did, she'd inadvertently drawn the eye of the enemy.

Her success had brought her out from under the radar. Instead of being irrelevant to the all-powerful Ferraras, she'd made herself significant. This was all her fault, she thought miserably. In pursuing her goal of providing for her family, protecting her son, she'd inadvertently exposed him.

'Fiammetta!'

Her grandfather's bark made her jump and she sprang to her feet and walked back towards the stone house that had been in the family for six generations, a feeling of sick dread in her stomach. *'Come stai?'* She kept her voice light. 'You're up late, Nonno. How are you feeling?'

'I'm as well as a man can be when he sees his granddaughter working herself to the bone.' He scowled down at the bottle in her hand. 'A man doesn't like to see a woman drinking beer.'

'Then it's a good job I don't have a man I need to worry about.' She teased him lightly, relieved that he had the energy to spar with her. This was their relationship. This was Baracchi love. She told herself that just because he didn't express it didn't mean he didn't feel it. On some days she actually believed that. 'What are you doing up? You should be asleep in bed.'

'Luca was crying.'

'He had a dream. He just wanted a cuddle.'

'You should leave him to cry.' Her grandfather gave a grunt of disapproval. 'He'll never grow up to be a man the way you coddle him.'

'He's going to be a fine man. The best.'

'The boy is spoiled. Every time I see him, someone is hugging him or kissing him.'

'You can't give a child too much love.'

'Did I fuss over my son the way you fuss over yours?'

No, and look at how that turned out. 'I think you should go to bed, Nonno.'

'Can I cook for a few people? That's what you said to me—' he winced as he walked stiffly towards the waterfront

'—and before I know it my home is full of strangers and you are serving good Sicilian food on fancy plates and lighting candles for people who wouldn't know the difference between fresh food and fast food.'

'People travel a long way to taste my cooking. I'm running a successful business.'

'You shouldn't be running a business.' Her grandfather settled himself in his favourite chair at the water's edge. The chair he'd sat on when she was a child.

'I'm building a life for myself and a future for my child.' A life that was now overturned. A future that was threatened. Suddenly she didn't trust herself not to betray what she was feeling. 'I'll fetch you a drink. *Grappa*?'

She had to tell her grandfather about Santo, but first she had to work out how. How did you tell someone that the father of his precious great-grandchild was a man he hated above all others?

Fia walked back to the kitchen and grabbed the bottle and a glass. It was a long time since he'd mentioned the Ferraras. And that was because of her, of course. Concerned for Luca, she'd insisted that if he couldn't speak the name positively then he wasn't to speak the name at all.

At first she was just grateful that he'd taken her threat seriously, but now she was wondering whether it meant he'd actually softened over time.

Please. Please let him have softened—

Fia put the glass on the table in front of her grandfather and poured. 'So what's wrong?'

'You mean apart from the fact that you are here every night slaving in that kitchen while someone else looks after your child?'

'It's good for Luca to be with other people. Gina loves him.' She didn't have the family she wanted for her son, so she'd created it. Her son was never going to be lonely in the way she'd been lonely. He had people he could turn to. *People who would hug him when life threw rocks.*

'Love.' Her grandfather grunted with contempt. 'You are turning him into a girl. That's what happens when there is no father to teach a boy to be a man.'

It was the perfect opening for her to tell him what she needed to tell him. But Fia couldn't push the words past her dry throat. She needed time. *Time to discover what Santo intended to do.* 'Luca has male influences in his life.'

'If you're talking about that boy you employ in the restaurant, there's more testosterone in my finger than he has in his whole body. Luca needs a real man around.'

'You and I have very different ideas about what makes a real man.'

His bony shoulders slumped and the lines on his forehead were deep. In the past month he appeared to have aged a decade. 'This isn't what I wanted for you.'

'Life doesn't always turn out the way we plan it, Nonno. When life gives you olives, you make olive oil.'

'But you don't make olive oil!' He waved a hand in frustration. 'You send our olives to our neighbours and *they* make our oil.'

'Which I use in my restaurant. The restaurant that everyone in Sicily is talking about. I was in the paper last week.' But somehow the buzz that she'd got from that fleeting moment of success had gone. Recent events had diminished it to nothing. 'The week before I was mentioned in an important travel blog. The article was called "Sicilian Secrets". I'm doing well. I'm good at my work.'

'Work is what a woman does before she finds a husband.'

Fia put the bottle down on the table. 'Don't say that. Soon, Luca will be old enough to understand you and I don't want him growing up with that opinion.'

'Men ask you out! But do you say yes? No, you don't. Dark,

blond, tall, short—it's always "no". You shut everyone out and you have done since Luca's father.' He looked at her intently and Fia's fingers tightened on the bottle.

'When I meet a man I'm interested in, I'll say yes.' But she knew that wasn't going to happen. There had only ever been one man in her life and right now he despised her. And worse, he thought she was an unfit mother.

Barely able to think about that, she focused on her grandfather and felt a flicker of worry as she saw him absently rub his fingers across his chest. Impulsively, she reached across the table and touched his hand. When he immediately withdrew, she tried not to mind. Her grandfather wasn't tactile, was he? It was silly of her to even try. He didn't hug her and he didn't hug Luca. 'What's wrong? More pain?'

'Don't fuss.' There was a long silence while he glared at her and something in his gaze made her stomach clench.

Was it just her guilty conscience or did he—?

'You weren't going to tell me, were you?' The harshness of his voice shocked her and she felt as if the earth had shaken beneath her feet.

'Tell you what?' Her heart was suddenly pounding like a drum in a rock band.

'He was here tonight. Santo Ferrara.' He said it as if the name tasted bad on his tongue and Fia put the bottle down before it slipped from her hand.

'Nonno—'

'I know you banned me from mentioning his name but when a Ferrara walks onto my property, that gives me the right to talk about him. You should have told me he was here.'

How much did he know? How much had he heard?

'I didn't tell you because I knew this would be your reaction.'

He thumped his fist on the table. 'I warned that boy not to step onto my land again.'

Fia thought about the width and power of those shoulders. The haze of dark stubble accentuating that hard jaw. 'He's not a boy. He's a man.' A wealthy man who now ran a global corporation. A man with the power to shake up everything she loved about her life. A man who had gone off to talk to lawyers and think about the future of her son.

Their son.

Oh, God—

Her grandfather's eyes glowed bright with rage. 'That *man* walked into my home—*my home*—' he stabbed the air with his finger '—with no respect for my feelings.'

'Nonno—'

'Did he have the courage to face me?'

'*Calma*! Calm down.' Fia was on her feet; the emotion was a burning ball at the base of her ribs. If her grandfather was this upset now, how much worse was it going to be when he found out the truth? It was starting again, only this time Luca would be in the middle of it. 'I didn't want him to see you and this is why! You're getting upset.'

'Of course I am upset. How could I not be upset after what he has done?' His face was white in the flickering light from the candle and Fia was sure that hers was equally pale.

'You *promised* me when Luca was born that you would let the past go.'

He gave her a long, long look. 'Why are you defending him? Why is it that I'm not allowed to say a bad word about a Ferrara?'

Fia felt the heat pour into her cheeks. 'Because I don't want Luca growing up with that animosity. It's horrible.'

'I hate them.'

Fia breathed deeply. 'I know.' *Oh, yes, she knew.* And she'd thought about that every day since she'd felt the first fluttering low in her abdomen. She'd thought about it as she'd pushed her son from her body, when she'd first looked into his eyes and every time she kissed him goodnight. There were days when she felt as if she couldn't carry the weight of it any more.

Her grandfather's eyes were fierce. 'Because of Ferrara, you will be alone in the world when I'm gone. Who will look after you?'

'I will look after us.' She knew he blamed Santo for her brother's death. She also knew it was pointless to remind him that her brother had barely been able to look after himself, let alone another. It had been his own reckless irresponsibility that had killed him, not Santo Ferrara.

Her grandfather rose unsteadily to his feet. 'If Ferrara dares to come back here again and I'm not around you can give him a message from me—'

'Nonno—'

'—you can tell him I'm still waiting for him to act like a man and take responsibility for his actions. And if he dares set foot on my property again I'll make him pay.'

CHAPTER THREE

Santo sat and waited in his office at the Ferrara Beach Club—an office hastily vacated in his honour by the manager of the hotel. If he needed an indication as to why this hotel was less successful than the others in the group it was right there on the desk. Lack of discipline and organisation was visible everywhere, from the scattered papers to the dying plant that drooped sadly in the corner of the office. Later, he'd deal with it. Right now he had other things on his mind. Mocking him from the wall was an enlarged photograph of the hotel manager, posing with his wife and two smiling children.

A typical Sicilian family.

Santo stared moodily at that picture. Right now he felt like tearing it down. He'd never considered himself idealistic, but was it idealistic to assume that one day his family would look much like the one in the picture?

Apparently it was.

He glanced at his watch.

Not for one moment did he doubt that she would come. Not because he had faith in her sense of justice but because she knew that if she didn't, he'd come and get her.

His face expressionless, he waited as darkness gave way to the first fingers of dawn; as the sun rose over the sea, showering light across the smooth glassy surface.

He'd sent the text in the early hours, at a time when most

people would have been asleep. It hadn't occurred to him to try and sleep. There had been no rest for him and he knew there would have been none for her, either.

Exhaustion fogged his mind and yet his thoughts were clear. As far as he was concerned the decision was clear. If only the emotions were as simple to deal with.

He checked his phone again and found a message from his brother, another person who had been frequenting the early hours. Just four words—

What do you need?

Unconditional support. Unquestioning loyalty. All those things that a family should offer, and which his did. He'd been raised with that support, surrounded by love. Unlike his son, who had spent his early years in the equivalent of a pit of vipers.

Sweat beaded on his brow. He could barely allow himself to think about what his son's life must have been like. What was the long-term impact of being raised in an emotional desert? And what if the abuse hadn't just been emotional? Although he'd been young, he still remembered the mutterings and the rumours about the Baracchi family. Remembered seeing Fia sporting bruises almost all the time.

The knock on the door was the most reluctant sound he'd ever heard.

His eyes narrowed and he felt a rush of adrenaline, but it was only a young chef from the kitchen, bringing him more coffee.

'Grazie—'

The rattle of the cup on the saucer and her nervous glance told him that his black mood was visible on his face although they'd probably all misinterpreted the cause. Everyone in the hotel from the top down was jumpy about his visit. Normally they'd have reason. They had no way of knowing that his current mood was caused by something different. That a reorganization of the hotel was the last thing on his mind right now.

She melted away but moments later there was another tap on the door and he knew instantly that this time it was her.

The door opened and Fia stood there, those fierce green eyes glittering like jewels in a face as pale as morning mist. One look at her white face told him that she hadn't had any more rest than he had.

She looked washed out and stressed. *And ready for a fight.*

Across the room their eyes clashed.

They'd been lovers.

They'd shared the ultimate intimacy, but that wasn't going to help them navigate the treacherous waters they now found themselves in because they'd shared nothing else. They had no relationship. Essentially they were strangers. All they'd had were a few chance encounters and one stolen night, one delicious taste of the forbidden. None of that was going to help them through this desperate situation. And it *was* desperate; even he could see that.

'Where is my son?' He snapped out the words and she leaned her back against the door and looked at him.

'Asleep in his bed. In his home. And if he wakes, Gina is there, and my grandfather.'

The anger rushed at him like a ravenous beast ready to snap through the last threads of his fragile self-control. 'And that is supposed to provide me with comfort?'

'He loves Luca.'

'I think we have a very different idea of what that word means.'

'No.' Her eyes were fierce. 'No, we don't.'

Santo's mouth tightened. 'And will he still "love" him when he discovers the identity of his father? I think we both know the answer to that.' He rose from his chair and saw her hand shoot towards the door handle. His mouth tightened and his eyes narrowed in a warning. 'If you leave this room then we will be having this conversation in public. Is that what you want?'

'What I want is for you to calm down and be rational.'

'Oh, I'm rational, *tesoro*. I have been thinking clearly from the moment I saw my child.'

The atmosphere thickened. The air grew overly warm.

'What do you want me to say? That I'm sorry? That I did the wrong thing?' Her voice was smoky-soft and that voice drew his eyes to the smooth column of her throat and then to her mouth. It had been just one night but the memory of it had left deep scars in his senses. He knew how she'd taste because he remembered it vividly. He knew how she'd feel because he remembered that too. Not just the smooth texture of her skin, but the softness of her gorgeous hair. Now released from the clips that had restrained it during cooking, it fell down her back like a dark flame, reflecting the sunrise back at him. He remembered the day her father had cut it short in a blaze of Baracchi temper, hacking with kitchen scissors until she'd been left with a jagged crop. A horrified Santo had witnessed the incident and had tried to intervene but the sight of him had simply inflamed the situation.

She'd sat still, he remembered, saying nothing as hunks of long hair had landed in her lap. Afterwards she'd hidden in the boathouse, her fierce glare challenging him to say one word about it and of course he hadn't because their relationship didn't encompass verbal exchanges.

And it had been in the boathouse, on that one night that had ended so tragically, that their relationship had shifted from nothing to everything.

Santo hauled in a deep breath, resisting that savage, elemental instinct that had him wanting to flatten her to the wall and drag the answers from her. 'When did you find out you were pregnant?'

'Why does that matter?'

'I'm the one asking the questions and right now you'll answer any question I choose to ask you.'

She closed her eyes and leaned her head back against the door. 'Not for ages. Afterwards…I can't really remember. It's all a blur. First there was the hospital. Then the funeral. And my grandfather…' Her sudden silence said more than words. Her breathing was fractured. 'It was chaos. The last thing I was thinking about was me.'

Yes, it had been chaos. Pandemonium. A huge tangled mess of blame, guilt, regret and raw emotion. The frantic rush to save a life that was already lost. A moment of intimacy lost in a sea of negative publicity and cruel gossip. Remembering it sent the tension flowing through his muscles and he knew she was feeling the same. In fact he was fairly sure that the only thing holding her upright was willpower.

'So when *did* you find out?'

'I don't know. I suppose it must have been a couple of months. Longer—' she rubbed her fingers over her forehead '—it was a very difficult time. I probably should have realised sooner but at the time I just thought that everything I was feeling was part of the shock. I felt sick the whole time but I thought that was grief. And when I did finally work it out it seemed like—'

'—one more problem?' His hands were clenched by his sides but her eyes flew to his, appalled.

'No!' She shook her head violently. 'I was going to say that it seemed like a miracle.' Her words dropped to a whisper. 'The best thing in my life came from the worst night of my life.'

It wasn't the response he'd expected and for a moment it threw him. 'When you realised, you should have contacted me.'

'For what purpose?' There was despair in her tone. 'So

that you and my grandfather could rip each other to pieces? Do you think I wanted Luca exposed to that? I made the decision that was best for my baby.'

'*Our* baby,' Santo corrected her with lethal emphasis. 'And from now on we'll be making those decisions together.' He saw the panic flicker across her face and knew that anxiety was responsible for those dark shadows under her eyes.

'Luca is happy. I can understand how you're feeling, but—'

'You do not understand how I'm feeling.' His voice was raw. Savage. He didn't know himself and he certainly didn't trust himself. 'This is my son we're talking about. Did you honestly believe I would want him to grow up a Baracchi?' He braced himself to ask the question that had robbed him of sleep. 'Has he ever hit him?'

'No!' Her denial was immediate and sincere. 'I would never, ever allow anyone to touch Luca.'

'And how do you defend him? You never defended yourself.' Perhaps it was low of him, but he told himself that his son's welfare was more important than her feelings. 'You just endured it.'

'I was eight years old!' Hurt and reproach flickered in her eyes and suddenly he felt like an animal for ripping into her. That was what people had done all their lives, wasn't it?

'I apologise for that remark,' he breathed and she shook her head.

'You don't need to. I don't blame you for being protective of your child.' She spoke quietly, as if she had long since resigned herself to the fact that no one had any concern for her. 'And yes, I was brought up in a violent family but that violence came from my father, not my grandfather. I assure you that Luca has never been at risk. He has had a warm, loving childhood.'

'Without a father in his life.'

She flinched as if he'd slapped her. 'Yes.'

'Naturally I am relieved that he has been safe, but that doesn't change the fundamental issue here. Family is the most important thing to me. I am a Ferrara and we look after our own. There are no circumstances—*none*—that would induce me to walk away from my own child.' His words struck another blow because of course her mother had done exactly that. She'd walked away when Fia was only eight years old.

Her face lost the last hint of colour and he wondered briefly how it must feel to watch a parent walk away, leaving you to cope with danger alone.

He knew the story, as did everyone else. Her mother had been an English tourist who had fallen for the charms of the smooth, good-looking Pietro Baracchi, only to discover after the wedding that he was an incurable womanizer with a dangerous temper. After one beating too many, she'd turned her back on Sicily and her two children and soon after that Fia's father had been killed in a drunken boating accident.

She watched him steadily. 'You are very quick to judge me, but did you bother to come back and find out if there were consequences to our night together?'

Her unexpected attack shook him. 'I used contraception.'

'And that worked out well, didn't it?' She tilted her head. 'Did you, at any point, wonder how I was doing after that night? How I was coping after the accident that killed my brother? Did you bother to come and find me?'

'I did not wish to inflame the situation.' But her words had kindled a nagging guilt. He should have contacted her. The thought was uncomfortable, like walking with a sharp stone in your shoe.

'So you're admitting your concern that having contact with me would escalate our problems.' Her voice was remarkably calm. 'How much more inflammatory would it have been if I'd told you there was a child?'

'The child changes everything.'

'It changes nothing. It just makes everything harder.' She pushed her hands into the pockets of her jeans. With a face free of make-up and her hair loose, she looked impossibly young. More like a teenager than a successful business-woman. 'It's a waste of time dwelling on what is already done so let's talk about the future. Of course you want to see him. I understand that. We can arrange something.'

Distracted by the length of her legs in those jeans, Santo frowned. 'What's that supposed to mean?'

'I'm saying that you can see Luca. We'll work something out, providing you agree to certain rules.'

She was giving *him* rules? Stunned, he could barely respond. 'What rules?'

'I will not at any time tolerate you speaking ill of my grandfather in front of Luca. Nor will you denigrate anyone else in my family, and that includes me. No matter how angry you are with me, you will not show it in front of Luca. As far as he is concerned, we are united. We might not be together, but I want him to believe we are on friendly terms. Providing you agree to that then I'll let you have full access.'

Genuinely shocked at the depth of her misunderstanding, Santo felt exasperation surge through him. 'Access? You think I am talking about visiting rights? You think this is about making polite arrangements to take my child on the occasional outing?'

'Don't you want that?'

'*Sì*, I want access. Full access.' His tone was a perfect reflection of his mood. Grim. 'The sort of access that comes from being a full-time father. Access to tuck him in at night and get him up in the morning. Access to spend all the time I want to spend with him. Access to teach him what family is *truly* about. And that is what is going to happen. I have had lawyers working through the night drawing up the necessary paperwork to acknowledge him as my son. *My* son.'

There was a hideous silence.

For a moment she said nothing and then she exploded across the room like a wild thing and pounded his chest with her fists.

'You will *not* take him from me! I won't let you.' She was so furious and he was so shocked by the unexpected explosion of emotion it took him a few seconds to grasp those slender wrists, a few more seconds to free himself from a lock of that vivid hair that had wrapped itself around him.

'And yet you took him from me—' He enunciated every syllable, threw those words right into her shocked face and saw the exact moment reality sank home.

'I'm his mother—' her voice was hoarse '—I will not let you take him. I will find a way of stopping you. He needs me.'

Santo paused long enough to make her suffer a fraction of what he had suffered since he'd discovered the truth. Then he released her hands and stepped away from her. 'If you're trying to impress me with your maternal dedication then don't waste your time. Even if everything else you say is true, the fact is that you have employed a nanny.'

She stepped back from him, confusion on her face. 'What does Gina have to do with this?'

'You don't look after him yourself.'

'I do look after him—' her eyes were stricken '—and there are reasons I choose to have a nanny. I can—'

'You don't have to explain. Caring for a child full-time is a demanding experience. A young child is very restricting, as your mother discovered. She chose to walk away from it. I'm willing to give you the opportunity to do the same.'

Her eyes were huge. 'I don't understand what you're saying.'

'I'm saying that I will take full responsibility for him.'

'You're…threatening to take my son from me?'

'Offering,' Santo interjected smoothly, watching her face closely. 'Offering, not threatening. And if you want to see him then of course that can be arranged.'

Her breathing was shallow. 'You think I want to give him away?'

'You can have your life back. And given that I'm prepared to sweeten the deal with a significant financial incentive, it could be a very comfortable life. It's a generous offer. Take it. You'd never have to work again.'

She lifted her hands to her cheeks and gave a choked laugh. 'You really don't know anything about me, do you? I love my son, and if you truly believe for a moment that I'd give him to you on any terms then you have no idea who you're dealing with.' Her hands dropped to her sides. Clenched into fists. 'There's nothing I wouldn't do to protect my child.'

Unmoved by the anger in her eyes, Santo nodded. 'Your mother would have taken the money and run. It's to your credit that you didn't do the same.'

'So this was some sort of test?' She gave a moan of disgust. 'You're sick, do you know that?'

'Our child's future is at stake. There is nothing I wouldn't do to protect him. If protecting him means offending you, I'll do that too.' He threw her own words back at her and she wrapped her arms around herself.

'I am not my mother. I will never leave Luca.'

'In that case we will find another solution.' And there was only one that he could see. He consoled himself with the fact that at least she was making an effort to fight for her child.

'Do you think I haven't searched for one?' Her raw tone exposed layers of despair. 'There *is* no solution. I don't want him shuttled between us. I don't want him absorbing all the bad feeling that runs between our families. He's been brought up in an atmosphere of happiness and calm.'

'Knowing your grandfather, I find that impossible to believe.'

'My grandfather has stuck to my rules.'

Santo frowned. 'More rules?'

'Yes. From the moment Luca was born, I insisted that any mention of the name Ferrara in our house had to be positive. I didn't want my son growing up in the same poisonous atmosphere I experienced.'

Genuinely surprised, Santo lifted his eyebrows. 'And how did you achieve this miracle of good behaviour?'

'I threatened to take his grandson away unless he agreed to my terms.'

If he'd been surprised before, he was shocked now. *So she was stronger than she looked, then.* 'Ingenious.'

'You will abide by the same rule. You will not speak badly about my family in front of Luca. If you can't say anything nice, then you don't mention us. When he spends time with you I want to be confident that you are not denigrating my family and I *will* know because right now Luca is like a recording device. He repeats everything he hears.'

Fascinated that so much passion could be trapped in such a small package and reluctantly impressed at her steadfast refusal to involve herself in the Baracchi/Ferrara hostilities, Santo took his time to respond.

'Firstly,' he said softly, 'the bad feeling was all on your side. We made several overtures, all of which were rejected. Secondly, you will know what I am saying to Luca because you will be there to hear it in person. Thirdly, our families will be merged, so all this ceases to be relevant.'

'Merged?' Nervous, she pushed her hair back from her face. 'You mean because Luca belongs to both of us?'

'I mean because I intend to marry you.'

Silence spread across the room.

For a moment he wondered if she'd actually heard him.

Then she made a strange sound in her throat and took a step backwards.

'*Marry* you?' Her voice was barely audible. 'You have to be joking.'

'Relish the moment, *tesoro*. Up until now, women have waited in vain for a proposal of marriage from me.'

She looked as if she'd suffered a major shock. 'You're proposing.'

'In a practical sense, yes. In a romantic sense, no,' he drawled, 'so if you're expecting me to get down on one knee you can forget it.'

This, he thought, would be a real test of her devotion to their son.

She lifted her hand to her throat and looked at him as if he was mad. 'Apart from the fact that we haven't laid eyes on each other for three years and barely know each other, there is no way our families would accept this.'

'I presume you are talking about your side of the family, because my side will support me in whatever decision I make. That's what families do. The reaction of yours is of no interest to me.' He gave an indifferent shrug. 'And as for the fact that we barely know each other, that will be rectified quickly enough. You will get to know me fast enough because I don't intend to let you out of my sight.'

She sleepwalked to the window. 'I saw a picture of you just last week strolling along a red carpet with a woman on your arm—you have a million women chasing after you.'

'Then it's fortunate for you that I was waiting for that one special person and hadn't yet made that commitment.' His expectations mocked him. His brother and his sister both had strong, happy marriages. He'd had no reason to believe that his wouldn't be the same. His hopes for the future were undergoing a transformation so rapid that it left him reeling.

'I can't accept your proposal.' Her voice had lost some of its strength. 'I don't need to. I run a successful business and—'

'This isn't about you, it's about Luca. Or does your streak of selflessness only emerge when it suits you? If you truly have Luca's best interests at heart then you will do what is right for him.' He came right back at her, offering no soft words of reassurance and she shook her head frantically.

'It would be wrong for Luca, too.'

'What's "wrong" is my child growing up in a family that doesn't know the meaning of the word,' he said coldly. 'He is a Ferrara and he is entitled to all the love and security that comes with being a Ferrara. And I am going to use every means at my disposal to make sure he is given that right.'

'You're doing this to punish me.' Her eyes were horrified. She knew how much power he wielded. She knew exactly what he could achieve if he set his mind to it. He saw her mind going to all sorts of places and he let it happen because it suited his purpose to scare her.

'Luca deserves to be raised in a strong, solid family, not that I expect you to understand that.' Another low blow and to her credit she didn't flinch from it.

'I do understand that. I understand that an ideal family is a unit of people who love and support you unconditionally. I admit I didn't have that, so I created it. I wanted Luca to be surrounded by people who would love him and support him and in reality I did need help because I wanted to be able to support us financially and not rely on my grandfather.'

'That is the most convoluted justification for a nanny I've ever heard.'

'You are very disparaging about nannies, but that is because you have aunts and cousins who all help each other with childcare. I don't have that and so I found a warm, loving girl I trust. She's been with us since Luca was born, and so has Ben because I wanted him to have a good male role

model—' She bit her lower lip. 'I'm aware that my grandfather isn't soft or tactile. He never hugs and I wanted Luca
to be hugged. I wanted him surrounded by people who felt
like I did. People who would give him affection. I didn't have
a family like yours, but I tried to create one for him.'

She'd *created* a family?

Santo thought about what he'd seen. About the amount of
affection he'd witnessed in that short time with his son. 'If
that is true, then that is definitely a point in your favour, but
it is no longer necessary. Luca doesn't need a stand-in family. He can have the real thing.'

'You're not thinking straight.' Her voice was remarkably
strong. 'My father married my mother because he made her
pregnant. I was first-hand witness to the fact that approach
doesn't work. And now you are suggesting we do the same
thing?'

'*Not* the same thing.' He heard the chill in his own voice.
'Our marriage will be nothing like your parents', I can assure
you of that. They led separate lives and their children—*you*—
were the casualties of their selfish, hubristic existence, not to
mention the vicious Baracchi temper. Our marriage will not
be like that.'

She rubbed her fingers over her brow and gave him a desperate look. 'You are angry and I don't blame you for that,
but please, please think of Luca.'

'I have thought of nothing but Luca since I walked into
your kitchen last night.'

'How can he possibly benefit from you and I being together? You are being hasty—'

'Hasty?' Just thinking about how much of his son's life he'd
missed made him want to punch his fist through something.
'As far as I'm concerned we are long past "hasty". Luca has
an aunt and an uncle. Cousins to play with. He has a whole
family he knows nothing about.' Seeing the wistfulness in

her eyes, he drove his point home. 'As a Ferrara he will never feel lonely or unloved. He will never have to hide in an abandoned boathouse because his family is in crisis.'

'You bastard—' She whispered the words, her eyes two deep pools of pain, but Santo was impervious to any emotion but anger.

'You hid my child from me. You robbed him of the right to a warm, loving family and you robbed me of something that can never be returned. Do I intend to dictate terms from now on? Yes, I do. And if that makes me a bastard I'll happily live with that title. Think about it.' He strode towards the door. 'And while you're thinking, I have work to do.'

'You're going to *work*?'

'Of course. I have a company to run.'

She shook her head in disbelief. 'I…I need some time to decide what is best for Luca.'

Holding on to his temper, Santo yanked open the door. 'Having a father and joining the Ferrara family is what is best for Luca and even twisted Baracchi thinking will struggle to distort that fact. You have until tonight to see sense. And I suggest you tell your grandfather the truth, or I'll do it for you.'

CHAPTER FOUR

THERE was nothing quite so cruel as the distortion of a dream.

How many times had she stared across the bay and envied the family life of the close-knit Ferraras? How many times had she wished she were part of that? It was no coincidence that in times of trauma she'd chosen to hide in their boathouse, as if simply by being there she might soak up some residual warmth.

She'd crawled through the open window, grazing her leg on the rough wood of the window frame, covering herself in dust as she'd landed. Fia hadn't cared about any of that.

With the sea lapping at the door that conveniently faced away from the bay, she had no fear that someone would find her. Who would look for her here, in the enemy camp? So sure had she been of the seclusion of her hiding place that when she'd seen Santo standing on the rocks, watching her, she'd known a moment of pure terror. Too afraid even to breathe, she'd waited for him to blow her cover. Her family hated his. Even a mention of the Ferrara name was enough to sour the atmosphere in her house for days. The only thing the Baracchi family knew how to nurture was a grudge.

And so she'd waited for Santo Ferrara to blow her cover.

Not only had he not done that, but he'd left her alone, as if understanding her need for space.

To her eight-year-old eyes, he'd turned from a boy she'd

envied into something close to a god. The boathouse became her regular hiding place and from there she could observe the Ferraras and see the differences between their family and her own. Suspicion turned to wistful envy. She'd envied the family picnics, their games on the beach. It was from them she'd learned that a quarrel could be affectionate, that a father could embrace a child, that a sister and brother could be close, *that a family could be a unit*.

Some of the girls at school had joked about discovering that they were secretly a princess. Fia's childhood dream was to wake up one day and discover that she was secretly a Ferrara; that there had been some mix-up at the hospital and somehow she'd ended up in the wrong family. That one day they'd claim her.

Be careful what you wish for.

Her head throbbing from lack of sleep, her stomach churning from an encounter she'd found hideously stressful, Fia dragged her mind back to the present and tried to work out what to do next. She had until tonight to find a way to tell her grandfather that the man he hated above all other was Luca's father.

Once she'd negotiated that hurdle she'd move on to the next one. How to respond to Santo's 'proposal' of marriage.

The suggestion was utterly ridiculous.

What sane woman would agree to marry a man who felt the way Santo felt about her?

On the other hand she could hardly criticise him for fighting for his child when her whole life had been spent wishing that her parents had done that for her. How could she argue with his claim that her son deserved to be a Ferrara when she'd modelled her little family on them?

If she agreed to his terms then Luca would grow up a

Ferrara. He'd have the life she'd craved as a child. He would be cocooned in a warm and loving family, wrapped up in love.

And for that privilege she would have to pay a very high price.

She would have to join the family too, only unlike her son she would never truly be part of it. She would be tolerated, rather than welcomed. She'd be on the outside.

And she'd spend every day of her life with a man who didn't love her. Who was furious with the decision she'd made.

How was that good for Luca?

It wasn't.

Somehow she had to make Santo understand that no one would benefit from such an arrangement.

Mind made up, she arrived back at the Beach Shack to find the kitchen a hive of activity. Life was the only thing that could fall apart and yet still carry on, she thought numbly. She should have been relaxed, here in her tiny slice of paradise with the sparkling Mediterranean Sea lapping at the shore just steps away from her, but she'd never felt more stressed in her life.

'Hey, Boss, I wondered where you were. I met the boat this morning. Beat everyone to it. The *gamberi* look good—' Ben was hauling a box of supplies into the kitchen. 'I've put them on the menu. *Gamberi e limone con pasta*?' He caught her expression and frowned. 'But if you'd rather do something else then just tell me.'

'It's fine.' Functioning on automatic, she checked the quality of the fruit and vegetables that had been delivered by her local suppliers. It was as if nothing had changed, and yet everything had changed. 'Did the avocados arrive?'

'Yes. They look perfect. It was a good idea to switch.' He paused with a box clutched to his chest. 'So, are you OK?'

He wasn't really asking that, of course. He was asking

what had happened with Santo and she wasn't ready to discuss that with anyone. 'Where is my grandfather?'

'Still in the house, I think. Oh, and Luca has a new word—' he was grinning at her '—*gamberi*. Gina and I took him down to the quay this morning while they were unloading the boat. He was fascinated by the octopus. Wanted to take it home. Which we did. But we didn't tell him we'd be cooking it and serving it with wine later.'

She managed a smile. Luca had grown up surrounded by these people. He was happy and confident. He'd witnessed none of the emotional fireworks that had scorched her childhood. Her heart ached to think that the simplicity of his life had gone for ever.

And just as she had that thought, Ben frowned over her shoulder.

'He's early for lunch, isn't he? And overdressed.'

Fia looked round and saw a bulky man in a suit hovering at the edge of her restaurant.

Her temper flared. Santo had promised her until tonight but already he was making his presence felt. 'Carry on, Ben,' she said quickly. 'I'll deal with this.' She had her phone in her hand and was dialling as she walked. 'Put me through to Ferrara—I don't care if he's in a meeting—tell him it's Fia Baracchi. Do it now…' Adrenaline coursed around her veins and she was ready to stalk right over there and smash her way into his precious meeting if she had to but moments later she heard his smooth masculine voice on the phone.

'This had better be important.'

'I have a man who looks like something straight from some mob movie prowling around my restaurant.'

'Good. That means he is doing his job.'

'And what exactly is his job?'

'He's in charge of security for the Ferrara Group. He's conducting a risk assessment.'

'A risk assessment?'

'Use your brain, Fia.'

From his curt tone she assumed he had people in the office with him and had no wish to broadcast his personal business. Soon the whole world would know, she thought numbly. They'd all know that Santo Ferrara had a son. And when that happened—

She wondered how he could concentrate in a meeting. She was so distracted she could barely string a coherent sentence together.

'I want him out of here. He'll frighten my customers.'

'The welfare of your customers is not my concern.'

Fia eyed the physical bulk and intimidating presence of the man currently exploring the perimeter of the restaurant and played the one card that was likely to influence him. 'He is going to frighten Luca.'

'Luigi is a family man and brilliant with children. And he's part of our deal. Now go and fulfil your part. Tell your grandfather or I'll do it myself. And don't ring me again unless it's urgent.' He hung up and Fia stalked over to the man, temper boiling, feeling as helpless as a fish trapped in a net.

'In two hours my restaurant will be full of customers. I don't want them thinking there is a problem.'

'As long as I'm here, there won't be a problem.'

'I don't want you here. You stand out. My guests will worry that something is going on. Luca is—' The fight went out of her and she swallowed. 'He's led a very low-profile life. I don't want him frightened.' She'd expected him to argue with her, to show the same rigid inflexibility as his arrogant boss, but to her surprise his eyes were sympathetic.

'I'm only here for his protection. If we can find a way to keep that low-key, that's fine by me.'

He knew the history. She could see it in his eyes and she lifted her chin, prepared to fight the whole world if she had to.

'I can protect my own son.'

'I know you think you can.' His voice was gruff. 'But he isn't just *your* son.' The implication was that it was the other half of the gene pool that mattered. If Luca had truly just been her son, he wouldn't have needed protection. Unfortunately his father was one of the most powerful men in Sicily and that bloodline made him a potential target for all sorts of unscrupulous individuals. The thought made her want to be sick.

'Is there really a risk?'

'Not with the security that Santo Ferrara has in place. Give me a minute to think about this—' He looked around the restaurant. 'We can work something out that keeps everyone happy.' His response was so unexpected that Fia felt emotion well up inside her.

Horrified, she gulped it down. 'I... Why are you being kind?'

'You gave my niece a job last summer when she had some trouble at home.' His voice was neutral. 'She had no experience, but you took her on.'

'Sabina is your niece?'

'My sister's child.' He cleared his throat. 'Why don't you give me the chair at the corner of the restaurant? I'll move a table to a position that works for me and I'll linger over my meal. That way I can blend with your customers and everyone is happy.'

Fia stared at him. 'And if he finds out?' There was no need to spell out who 'he' was.

'The boss doesn't micromanage his staff. He employs people he trusts and then lets them do their job in the way that best suits them.' He gave a faint smile. 'I wouldn't work for him if he didn't.'

Right now she didn't need to hear admiration in anyone's voice when they talked about Santo. But at least Luigi appeared reasonable. More reasonable than his boss.

'You can take that table—' agreeing to the compromise, she gestured '—and it would be great if you could take off your jacket. We're pretty casual here, especially at lunchtime.'

'Mamma!' Luca came sprinting through the restaurant and she heard Luigi's sudden intake of breath as he had his first glimpse of the child he'd been assigned to protect.

'Madre di Dio—'

The likeness was that obvious? Fia scooped her son into her arms protectively but he gazed curiously at the big man in the suit. He hadn't learned fear, she thought numbly. He'd been brought up here, by the beach, surrounded by people who loved him and guests who thought he was a charming addition to this hidden Sicilian gem. But once people knew he was Santo Ferrara's son, there would always be a risk. Even she could see that.

'This is Luigi,' she said huskily, 'and he is going to be eating in our restaurant today. Aren't we lucky?' She looked at the reassuring power house that was Santo's head of security and gave a slight smile. 'Thank you.'

'Figurati. You're welcome.' He winked at the boy and went to rearrange tables while Fia returned to her job.

A busy lunchtime merged into a crazy evening where she hardly emerged from the kitchen. She had time to check on her grandfather briefly, but no time to embark on a difficult conversation. It hung over her as she tossed gamberi into fresh pasta, and served her speciality dessert, Zuccotto al cioccolato. And all the time she was aware that time was running out.

By the time Gina and Ben had left for the night and everywhere was quiet, she was a nervous wreck.

All day she'd been rehearsing the best way to tell her

grandfather, trying to work out which combination of words would cause the least shock.

I need to talk to you about Luca.

You've often asked me about Luca's father...

Bracing herself for major conflict, she walked into the kitchen to finish her preparations for the next day and saw the frail figure of her grandfather crumpled on the floor.

'Nonno! *Cristo*, please, no!' She was across the floor and down on her knees in seconds, hands shaking as she gave his shoulder a gentle shake and then grabbed his thin wrist and tried to find a pulse. 'Speak to me— Oh, God, don't do this—' She scrabbled in her pocket for her phone and then realised she'd left it in the house.

'Is he breathing?' Santo's voice came from behind her, calm and strong as he strode across the room. His phone was already in his hand and he was talking into it, issuing a string of instructions in rapid Italian.

It was a measure of her stress that she was relieved to see him. She didn't even question what he was doing here. 'Did you call the emergency services? How long?'

'They're sending a helicopter.' With no hesitation, he moved her grandfather and pressed his fingers to the old man's neck. 'No pulse.'

Why had she felt his wrist and not his neck? She *knew* she was supposed to feel his neck but all her basic first aid knowledge had apparently been driven from her brain by panic. Unable to think properly, Fia took her grandfather's hand and rubbed it. 'Nonno—'

'He can't hear you.' Santo's voice was firm and steady. 'You need to move to one side so I can start CPR.'

'I'm not going anywhere!'

She heard someone running and then Luigi appeared in the kitchen holding a small box. 'Here, Boss—' He handed it to Santo, who moved with swift purpose and lightning speed.

'Undo his shirt, Fia.'

'But—'

'Just do it!' He yanked open the box and hit a switch.

'What are you doing?' Her fingers fumbled on buttons that didn't want to undo and she heard Santo mutter something in Italian and then strong hands were pushing hers aside and he tore the fabric and exposed her grandfather's chest in a single movement.

'Move away from him. Get back.' He ripped off the protective backing from two sticky pads and pressed them onto her grandfather's chest.

He just took control, she thought numbly, the way the Ferraras always took control. Not once did he hesitate or fumble.

'Do you even know how to use that thing?'

'It's an AED. And yes, I know how to use it.' He didn't spare her a glance. All his attention was focused on her grandfather as a disembodied voice delivered instructions from the machine.

Anxiety flared. 'You're going to give him a shock? But what if that's not the right thing to do? You might kill him!' And for a moment her own heart almost stopped because she realised that her grandfather's life was in the hands of a man who had no love for him.

His exasperated glance told her that he'd read her mind. 'This device contains a sophisticated computer chip. As far as I know, they're not programmed to bear grudges. Now let go of his hand.'

Reluctantly she moved back.

The voice instructed them to stand clear of the patient and press the button and after that the emergency services arrived and everything blurred. There was a flurry of activity while they stabilised her grandfather and then they transferred him swiftly into the air ambulance. And through it all she was aware of Santo, cool and in control. Santo, calling a top cardiologist and ordering him to meet them at the hospital. Santo arranging to drive her there. And when she pointed out that she had to take Luca and his Lamborghini wouldn't accommodate a child's car seat, he helped himself to Luigi's sturdy four-by-four instead. And Luca didn't even stir as she transferred him from bed to car seat, completely oblivious to the drama being played out around him.

'Does he have a favourite toy or something?' Santo secured the belt. 'Something he can't be without?'

She looked at him blankly and he gave an impatient sigh. 'My niece can't sleep without her favourite blanket. Does he have something like that?'

She swallowed. 'He sleeps with a stuffed giraffe.'

'Fetch it. It will help when he wakes up in a strange place.'

Wondering why he had been the one to think of that and not her, she sprinted to fetch Luca's giraffe and quickly stuffed a change of clothes for him into a bag.

Santo drove her himself and for once she was grateful for the tendency of Sicilians to drive too fast. They made the journey in silence and when he pulled up outside the Emergency Department he sat for a moment, his hands gripping the wheel as he stared at the double doors that led inside.

Fia undid her seat belt.

'They won't let you near him at the moment so there's no point in rushing. You might as well sit here for a while.' Santo switched off the engine. His expression was grim and there were lines of fatigue around his eyes. 'The waiting is the worst part.'

She was about to ask how he knew that when she remembered that his father had died suddenly of a heart attack. Had he been brought to this hospital? Staring at Santo's white knuckles, she assumed the answer to that was positive.

'Are you all right?' Her voice faltered because even to her

it sounded like a ridiculous question. Her grandfather was lying in the hospital and she was asking him if he was all right. And why would he even tell her? In all ways but one he was a stranger, except that no stranger ever made her feel the way that being close to him made her feel.

Even now, in these direst of circumstances, she felt that dangerous heat spread through her body. That awareness that made her skin prickle and her stomach flip.

He didn't speak and his silence unsettled her more than his anger had.

'I owe you thanks.' Embarrassment made her rigidly polite. 'For the lift and…and for your first aid skills. I'm grateful you arrived when you did, although I've no idea what you were doing there—' And then suddenly she knew.

He'd arrived ready to carry out his threat to tell her grandfather.

The reminder that she still had to do that made her feel sick.

'I gather he didn't take the news well.' His tone was flat and it took her a moment to understand that he thought her grandfather's heart attack was somehow related to their situation.

'I hadn't told him. I was going to. I'd just walked in and he was lying there. I panicked—' And that made her angrier than anything. Angry with herself. 'I don't know how I could have been so useless. I've done a first aid course. I should have known what to do.'

'It's different when it's someone you love.'

Were his words intended as comfort or statement of fact? Statement of fact, obviously. They didn't have the sort of relationship that allowed comfort.

That didn't stop her knowing what she owed him. 'How come you had one of those machines?'

'The AED? We have them in all our hotels. One at reception, one in the health and fitness clubs. Sometimes one on the golf course. Our staff are trained in CPR as part of their induction programme. You never know when they could save a life.' There was something in his voice that made her look closely at him but his profile revealed no clues as to his thoughts.

'Santo—'

'On second thought, why don't we go and see if there is someone who can give us an update.' Cutting across her, he opened the car door and then frowned as he realised Luca was asleep. 'There is no sense in disturbing him. Luigi can stay with him and let us know the moment he wakes.' He strode over to the other car and, after a brief exchange, Luigi eased his muscular bulk into the seat beside Luca.

'Don't you worry. If the little one so much as moves a muscle, I'll call you. You concentrate on your grandfather.'

Torn by her responsibilities, Fia allowed Santo to lead her into the Emergency Department.

As they walked through the glass doors she heard the breath hiss through his teeth. Even a brief glance was enough for her to see the tension in those wide shoulders. And this time she was sure that he was thinking about his father.

Of course she knew none of the details. Just that it had been sudden and that it had devastated the close-knit Ferrara family. Santo had still been at school, his older brother Cristiano away at university in the US. She'd seen pictures of the funeral in the paper, but she hadn't attended. A Baracchi wouldn't have been allowed within the charmed perimeter of the Ferrara circle but that didn't mean she hadn't felt his pain. It had seemed grossly unfair to her young mind that such a perfect family could suffer such a loss. Their father adored his three children. How was it right that he should die before his time?

And now Santo was back here, forced into it by grim circumstances.

The sight of a Ferrara in the hospital was enough to throw the staff into a frenzy. The top cardiologist had summoned his team and it was obvious from the flurry of activity that no expense or effort was being spared in the drive to save her grandfather.

Her brother had been jealous of that, she remembered bleakly. The ability of the rich, powerful Ferrara brothers to open doors with just one look. He'd wanted that for himself. What he hadn't understood was that their wealth and status had been achieved by hard graft. They didn't demand the respect of others, they earned it.

And in this instance she was grateful for their power and influence. It meant she had the best people taking care of her grandfather.

The exchange with the cardiologist was brief, but it was enough to confirm what she'd suspected—that her grandfather was alive because Santo had shocked his heart back into normal rhythm. That knowledge added to the confusion in her brain. She didn't want to be in debt to him, but at the same time part of her was proud that her son's daddy was a man who could save a life.

They were shown to a small room reserved for relatives and something about those impersonal, clinical surroundings increased her feeling of desolation. And perhaps he felt it too because he didn't sit, but instead stood with his back to her, staring out of the window at the chaos of the city.

Fia waited for him to leave and when he didn't her good opinion started to fade. Resentment grew with each passing moment. 'You don't have to stay. Even if he recovers, he won't be in a position to listen to you for a while.'

He turned. 'You think I'm staying so that I can tell him

the news? You think I'm that inhumane?' The ferocity in his voice shocked her.

'I assumed… Then why are you here?'

Incredulous dark eyes swept her face. 'Do you have any other family to support you?'

He knew she didn't. Her family wasn't like his. Apart from her son, the sum total of her family was currently fighting for his life in the coronary care unit.

'I don't need support.'

'The man you have lived with all your life is through those doors struggling to stay alive and you don't need support? That is coping with hard times the Baracchi way. Or should I say the Fia way.' He dragged his hand over the back of his neck and met her gaze. 'Maybe that's how you've dealt with them in the past but that isn't how you're going to deal with them in the future, be sure of that. I'm not leaving you here alone. From now on I'm by your side for all life's major events—births, deaths, the graduation of our children. And for the minor events, too. That's how we Ferraras conduct ourselves in a relationship. That's how it's going to be in *our* relationship, *tesoro*. Everything I said to you this morning still stands.'

The word 'relationship' reminded her that if her grand-father lived, she still had to break the news to him. And if he didn't—

Her heart felt as if someone was twisting it.

'You being here isn't support, Santo. It's adding to the stress because I know that you're just waiting to pick your moment to tell him.' Suddenly she needed to get away from him. From the width of those powerful shoulders and the sheer force of his presence. He'd made it his mission to eject her from the comfortable safe place she inhabited and she felt as vulnerable as a small animal chased from its burrow. 'I need to check on Luca.'

'He is still asleep. If he wasn't, Luigi would have called me.'

'He might not want to bother you.'

'I would trust Luigi with my life.'

Fia thought about how kind his head of security had been earlier. He'd had a job to do and he'd done it, but he'd done it with a sensitivity that had surprised her. 'It's not about trust. It's about the fact Luca doesn't know him. I don't want him to wake up, find himself in a strange place and be scared.'

Those eyes frowned into hers and he was about to answer when the door opened and the consultant walked in.

Panic gripped her. 'My grandfather—?' Now that the moment had come she was almost too afraid to ask the question that had to be asked. As if by postponing it for a few seconds she could change reality. 'Is he—?'

'He had an occluded coronary artery. Without rapid treatment he would not be here now. It is without doubt your use of the AED that saved him in those first precious minutes.' The consultant carried on, talking about heart muscle, clots and drugs, angioplasty and future risk factors but all she heard was that her grandfather was still alive. The rest washed over her in a wave of jargon she didn't understand and didn't want to understand.

It was Santo who asked the relevant questions. Santo who discussed treatment options and truthfully she was grateful to him because once again her brain seemed to be working in slow motion.

Eventually all the questions were answered and the consultant nodded. 'He wants to see you. Normally I would refuse at this point because he needs rest but it's clear that something is causing him stress. He is very agitated and he needs to be reassured.'

'Of course.' Fia flew to the door but the consultant stopped her.

'It was Santo he asked for. He was quite specific about that. Your grandfather asked for Santo Ferrara.'

Fia felt her knees shake and she glanced at Santo in horror. 'No! Seeing you will upset him badly.'

'He is already upset. Apparently there are things he needs to say,' the consultant told them, 'so I think it might be helpful for him. But keep it brief and keep any stress to a minimum.'

Santo would tell him that Luca was his child.

How was that keeping stress to a minimum?

Apparently suffering from none of her doubts, Santo strode through the door. 'Let's do this.'

She shot after him. 'Please don't.' She kept her voice low. 'Whatever you think of me, don't do this. Please don't tell him yet. Wait until he's stronger.' She almost stumbled as she tried to keep up with him, panicking madly, unable to see a single way that this encounter was going to have a happy ending. Why was her grandfather asking to see him? At this stage he couldn't even know that it was Santo who had saved his life.

Reluctantly, she walked into the room and caught her breath at the sight of the machines and wires that dominated her grandfather's frail form.

For a moment she couldn't move and then she felt a warm strong hand close over hers and the reassuring squeeze of male fingers.

Shocked, Fia stood for a moment, distracted by the novel experience of being comforted.

And then she heard a sound from the bed and saw her grandfather's eyes open. And she realised Santo's touch wasn't about comfort, but manipulation.

Instantly she snatched her hand away. 'Nonno—' She tried to catch his eyes and reassure him but her grandfather wasn't looking at her. He was looking at Santo.

And Santo, being who he was, didn't flinch or look remotely discomfited.

'You gave us all a shock,' he drawled, approaching the bed with a confidence that suggested he was a welcome visitor.

'Ferrara—' her grandfather's voice was weak and shaky '—I want to know your intentions.'

There was a long pulsing silence and Fia shot Santo a pleading glance, but he wasn't looking at her. He dominated the room, the power of his athletic physique a cruel contrast to the fragility of the man in the bed.

'I intend to be a father to my son.'

Time stood still.

She couldn't believe he'd actually said that. 'I don't—'

'About time!' Her grandfather's eyes burned fiercely in his pale face. 'For years I have been waiting for you to do the right thing—not even allowed to mention your name in case she walked out—' He glared at Fia and then coughed weakly. 'What sort of a man makes a woman pregnant and then leaves her to cope alone?'

'The sort of man who didn't know,' Santo replied in a cool tone, 'but now intends to rectify that mistake.'

Fia barely heard his response. She was staring at her grandfather.

'What?' He snapped the words. 'You thought I didn't know? Why do you think I was so angry with him?'

She sank into the nearest chair. 'Well, because—'

'You thought it was because of a stupid piece of land. And because of your brother.' Her grandfather closed his eyes, his face pale against the hospital sheets. 'I don't blame him for your brother. I was wrong about a lot of things. Wrong. There. I said it. Does that make you happy?'

Fia's heart clenched. A lump formed in her throat. 'You shouldn't be talking about this now. It isn't the time.'

'Always trying to smooth things over. Always wanting

everyone to love each other and be friends. Keep an eye on her, Ferrara, or she'll turn your son into a wimp.' Her grandfather's frame was racked by a paroxysm of coughing and Fia fumbled for the buzzer. Within moments the room filled with staff but he waved them away impatiently, his eyes still on Santo. 'There's one thing I want to know before they pump me full of more drugs that are going to dull my mind—' his voice rasped '—I want to know what you're going to do now that you know.'

Santo didn't hesitate. 'I'm going to marry your granddaughter.'

CHAPTER FIVE

HE HATED hospitals.

Santo scrunched the flimsy plastic cup in his hand and dropped it into the bin.

The smell of antiseptic reminded him of the night his father had died and just for a moment he was tempted to turn on his heel and walk right out again.

And then he thought of Fia, keeping vigil over her grandfather, hour after hour. His anger was still running hot. He was furious with her. But he couldn't accuse her of not showing loyalty to her family. And he couldn't leave her alone in this place.

Cursing softly, Santo strode back towards the coronary care unit that brought back nothing but bad memories.

She was sitting by the bed, her hair a livid streak of fire against her ashen skin. Those green eyes were fixed on the old man as if by sheer willpower and focus she might somehow transmit some of her youth and energy to him.

He'd never seen a lonelier figure in his life.

Or perhaps he had, he thought grimly, remembering the first time he'd seen her in his boathouse. Some people automatically sought human company when they were upset. Fia had taught herself to survive alone.

He compared that to his own big, noisy family. He knew from experience that had it been a Ferrara lying in the hospital bed the room would have been bulging with concerned relatives, not just his brother and sister but numerous aunts, uncles and cousins all clucking and fussing.

'How's he doing?'

'They gave him a sedative and some other stuff. I don't know what. They say the first twenty-four hours are crucial.' Her slim fingers were curled around her grandfather's. 'If he wakes up now he'll be angry that I'm holding his hand. He's not great at the physical stuff. Never has been.'

Santo realised that this woman's whole life revolved around the man currently lying in the bed and the child fast asleep in his car.

'When did you last eat?' It was the automatic Ferrara response to all moments of crisis and he almost laughed at himself for being so predictable.

'I'm not hungry.' Her voice was husky and she didn't shift her gaze from her grandfather. 'In a minute I'll go and check on Luca.'

'I just checked him. He hasn't stirred. He and Luigi are both asleep.'

'I'll bring him in here and tuck him up on the chair. Then you can go home. Gina will come and I need to call Ben and ask him to cover tomorrow.'

Santo felt an irrational surge of anger. 'He doesn't need to. I've already sorted that out. My team will take over running the Beach Shack for the time being.'

Her spine tensed. 'You're taking advantage of this situation to take over my business?'

Santo held on to his own temper. 'You need to stop thinking like a Baracchi. This is not about revenge. I'm not taking over your business, just making sure you still have one to come home to. I assumed you didn't want to leave your grandfather's bedside to cook *calamari* for a bunch of strangers.'

Her cheeks were pale. 'I'm sorry.' Her gaze skated back to her grandfather. 'I *am* grateful to you. I just assumed—'

'Well, stop assuming.' Her fragility unsettled him. And it wasn't the only thing that unsettled him. The response of his body was equally disturbing. His feelings were entirely inappropriate for the surroundings. 'You can do no more here tonight. Your grandfather is going to sleep and it's not going to help anyone if you collapse. We're leaving now. I've told the staff to call me if there is any change.'

'I can't leave. It's too far to get back here again if something happens.'

'My apartment is only ten minutes from here. If something happens, I'll drive you. If we leave now you can still get some rest and my son can wake up in a proper bed.' He'd been trying not to think about that side of things, putting his own emotions on hold in order to maintain the delicate balance of a situation that could only be described as difficult.

Perhaps it was the logic of his argument. Perhaps it was the words 'my son'. Either way, she ceased arguing and allowed him to lead her away from the bedside to the car.

Ten minutes later Luca was tucked up in the centre of an enormous double bed in one of his spare bedrooms.

Santo watched as she spread pillows on the floor next to the bed. 'What are you doing?'

'Sometimes he rolls. I don't want him to fall onto the tiled floor,' she muttered. 'Do you have a baby alarm?'

'No. Leave the door open a crack. Then we'll hear him if he wakes.' Santo strode out of the room and she followed, her eyes tracing every detail of his apartment.

'Do you live alone?'

'You think I'm hiding women under the sofa?'

'I just mean it's very big for one person.'

'I like the space and the views. The balconies face over

the old part of the town, not that I think Luca will be that discerning. What can I get you to eat?'

'Nothing, thank you.' Restless and tense, she walked over to the doors that led to the balcony and opened them. 'Don't you keep these locked?'

'You're worrying about my security?'

'I'm worrying about Luca's security.' Biting her lip, she stepped onto the small area and ran her finger along the iron railings. Then she gauged the height of the balcony. 'This is a real hazard. Luca is two years old. His favourite pastime is climbing. He climbs anything and everything he can find. We're going to have to lock the doors to the balconies and remove the keys.' She was brisk and practical, but then she walked past him and he caught the scent of her hair. Flowers. She always smelt like flowers.

Irritated with himself for being so easily distracted, Santo followed her back into the apartment. This time her eyes were on the large sunken living room that formed the centrepiece of his luxurious apartment. 'You're worrying about the welfare of my white sofas? Don't. My niece has already spilled something unmentionable on them. I don't care. People are more important than things.'

'I agree. And I'm not thinking about your sofas, I'm thinking of Luca. More particularly, I'm thinking about the step down to your living room.'

'It's an architectural feature.'

'It's a trap for a fearless toddler. He's going to fall.'

Santo digested that. 'He walks perfectly well. We will teach him to be careful.'

'He gets enthusiastic and excited. If he sees something he wants, he runs. If he does that here, he'll trip and smash his head on your priceless Italian tiles.'

Santo spread his hands in a gesture of surrender. 'So this

place is not exactly child-proofed; I accept that. I will deal with it.'

'How? You can't exactly remodel the apartment, can you?'

'If necessary. And in the meantime I will teach him to watch the step.' He tried to hide his exasperation. However angry he was, he was well aware that she'd been through the most stressful twenty-four hours of her life and yet, apart from her visible panic when she'd found her grandfather, she hadn't shown any emotion. She was frighteningly calm. The little girl who had refused to shed a tear had grown into a woman with the same emotional restraint. The only sign that she was suffering was the rigid tension in her narrow shoulders. 'Are you always like this? It's a wonder Luca isn't a bundle of nerves, living with you.'

'One minute you accuse me of not taking good care of your son and then you accuse me of taking too much care. Make up your mind.' She picked up a slender glass vase and transferred it to a high shelf.

'I was not accusing you of anything. Just pointing out that you're overreacting.'

'You have no idea what it's like, living with an active toddler.'

Her words snapped something inside him. 'And whose fault is that?' Bitterness welled up and threatened to spill over. Afraid he might say something he'd later regret, Santo strode towards the kitchen, struggling with the intensity of his own emotions.

'I'm sorry.' Her voice came from the doorway.

'What for?' He dragged open a cupboard. 'Keeping my son from me or casting doubt on my abilities as a father?'

'I wasn't casting doubt. Just pointing out the hazards of having an active toddler in a bachelor pad.' She looked impossibly fragile standing there with her hair pouring over her shoulders in soft waves of wicked temptation.

He didn't want to feel anything but anger yet he was sufficiently self-aware to know that his feelings were much, much more complicated than that. Yes, the anger was there and the hurt, but mixed in with those emotions was a hefty dollop of something far less easy to define but equally powerful.

The same thing that had brought them together that night.

'We'll do what needs to be done, Fia.' He left the statement purposefully ambiguous and pulled plates out of the cupboard. 'We need to eat. What can I get you?'

'Nothing, thank you. I think I'll go to bed. I'll sleep with Luca. That way, if he wakes up he won't be frightened.'

Santo thumped a fresh loaf of bread in the centre of the table. 'Who is frightened, *tesoro*? You or him?' He sent her a black look. 'You think if you don't sleep in his bed you'll be sleeping in mine?'

Wide green eyes fixed on his face. Those eyes that said everything her lips didn't. The first time he'd caught her in the boathouse he'd seen misery and fear, but also defiance. Even though she hadn't said a word, he'd had no trouble reading the message. *Go on and tell. See if I care.*

He hadn't told.

And he knew she would have cared.

She showed nothing, and yet he knew she was a woman who felt everything deeply. He wouldn't have been able to list her favourite colour or whether she liked to read, but he'd never doubted the intensity of her emotions. He'd always sensed the passion in her, simmering beneath the silent surface. And eventually, of course, he'd felt it. Touched it. Tasted it. *Taken it.* He could clearly remember the feel of her bare skin under his seeking fingers, the scent of her as he'd kissed his way down her body, the flavour of her under his tongue.

Sexual arousal was instant and brutal.

He dragged his gaze from the wicked curve of her hips back to her face.

Those green eyes had gone a shade darker and her cheeks were flushed.

Santo strode over to the fridge and yanked open the door. Maybe he should just thrust his whole body into it, he thought savagely. He had a feeling that was the only way of cooling himself down.

He was about to pull out a dish of *caponata* when another memory revealed itself. Frowning, he let go of the dish. It wasn't true to say he knew nothing about her, was it? There *was* something he knew. His mouth tightening, he put the *caponata* back and removed *pecorino* and olives instead. Putting them on the table next to the bread, he gestured. 'Eat.'

'I've told you I'm not hungry.'

'I make it a personal rule only to resuscitate one person a day so unless you want me to force-feed you, you'll eat.' He tore off a hunk of bread, added a slice of *pecorino* and some olives and pushed the plate towards her. 'And don't tell me you don't like it. The fact that you love *pecorino* is one of the few things I *do* know about you.'

A tiny frown touched her smooth brow as she stared at the plate and then back at him.

Santo sighed. 'When you hid in the boathouse you always brought the same food.' For a moment he thought she wasn't going to respond.

'I didn't want to have to go home to eat.'

'You didn't want to go home at all.'

'I know.' She gave a strangled laugh and pushed the plate away. 'You do know this is ridiculous, don't you? Just about the only thing you know about me is that I like *pecorino* and olives. And all I know about you is that you like really fast, flashy cars. And yet you're suggesting marriage.'

'I'm not suggesting marriage. I'm insisting on marriage. Your grandfather approved.'

'My grandfather is old-fashioned. I'm not.' Her eyes lifted

to his. 'I run a successful business. I can support my son. We would gain nothing from marriage.'

'Luca would gain a great deal.'

'He would live with two people who don't love each other. What would he gain from that? You're punishing me because you're angry, but in the end you will be the one who suffers. We are not compatible.'

'We know we're compatible in the one place that counts,' Santo said in a raw tone, 'or we wouldn't be in this position now.'

Colour darkened her cheekbones. 'You may be Sicilian, but you are far too intelligent to truly believe that all a marriage takes is good sex.'

Santo took the chair opposite her. 'I suppose I should be grateful you're at least admitting it was good sex.'

'You're impossible to talk to.'

'On the contrary, I'm easy to talk to. I say what I think, which is more than you do. I won't tolerate silence, Fia. Marriages are about sharing. Everything. I don't want a wife who locks away her feelings, so let's get that straight now. I want all of you. Everything you are, you're going to give it to me.' Clearly she hadn't expected that response from him because she turned white.

'If that's what you want, then you really do need a different wife.'

There was a certain satisfaction in having flustered her. 'You've taught yourself to be that way. That's how you've survived and protected yourself. But underneath, you're not like that. And I'm not interested in the ice maiden. I want the woman I had in my boathouse that night.'

'That was… It was…' she stumbled over the words '…that wasn't me.'

'Yes, it was. For a few wild hours you lost control of this

persona you've constructed. That was the real you, Fia. It's the rest of this that is an act.'

'Everything about that night was crazy—' her fingers were curled into her palms '—I don't know how it started, but I do know how it ended.'

'It ended when your brother stole my car and wrapped it around a tree.' He'd hoped the direct approach might shake her out of her rigid control but apparently even the shock of his blunt comment couldn't penetrate that wall she'd built around herself.

'It was too powerful for him. He'd never driven anything like it before.'

'Neither had I,' Santo said icily. 'I'd only received it two days earlier.'

'That is a monumentally tactless and unfeeling thing to say.'

Then show some emotion. 'About as tactless and unfeeling as the wordless implication that I was in some way responsible for his death.'

There was a throbbing silence. 'I have never said that.'

'No, but you've thought it. And your grandfather thought it. You say you don't know me, so learn this about me right now—I'm not good with undercurrents or people who hide what they're really thinking and I sure as hell am not going to feed this damn feud that we've both grown up with. It ends here, right now.' The fire burned hot inside him, strengthening his resolve. 'If what you said to me this morning is true then I presume you want that, too.'

'Of course. But we can kill the feud without getting married. There is more than one way of being a family.'

'Not for me. My child will not grow up being shuttled from one parent to another. We've never talked about that night, so let's do it now. Whatever you're thinking, I want it out in the open, not gnawing holes in that brain of yours. You blamed me for the fact that he took the car. And yet you know what happened that night. I was with you. And we had other things on our mind, didn't we, *bellissima*?'

'I never blamed you.'

'Really?' His sardonic tone made her lift her head and look at him.

'Yes, really.'

He waited for her to elaborate but of course she didn't and that failure to break through her defences exasperated him because he wasn't a man who liked to fail. Jaw tense, he breathed deeply, his emotions at war with each other. 'It's late and you've had a hell of a night. One thing I know about toddlers is that they don't lie in just because adult life is collapsing around them. What time does he wake up?'

'Five.'

His working day frequently began at the same hour. 'If you're not going to eat, then get to bed. I'll lend you one of my shirts to sleep in.'

A faint smile touched the soft curve of her mouth. 'So you don't have a wardrobe full of slinky nightwear for overnight guests? The world would be disappointed to discover that.'

'I don't encourage overnight guests. They can grow roots fast.' He watched her steadily. 'This once, I'll let you retreat. Make the most of it because once we're married there will be no hiding. Be sure of that.'

'We're not getting married, Santo.'

'We'll talk about it tomorrow. But everything I said in my office still stands.'

'No, it doesn't. You were concerned that Luca had been harmed, but you can see now that he has had a happy childhood.'

'I admire your efforts to create the family you didn't have, but my son doesn't need paid employees to fill that role. He has the real thing. A family ready and willing to welcome him. He's a Ferrara and the sooner we make that legal the better for everyone.'

'Is it?' Her voice suddenly seemed to gain strength. 'Is it really better for him to be brought up by parents who are strangers?'

Santo's mouth tightened. 'We're not going to be strangers, *tesoro*. We're going to be as intimate as it's possible for a man and a woman to be. I'm going to rip down those barriers you've built. When you're with me you might as well be naked because there is going to be no hiding. Now get some sleep. You're going to need it.'

As intimate as it's possible for a man and a woman to be.

What was intimate about that cold, emotionless statement? He was blisteringly angry. Furious. How did he think they could achieve intimacy under those circumstances?

She wasn't going to marry him. It would be wrong.

Once he calmed down, he'd see sense. They'd come to an agreement about how to share Luca. And perhaps the three of them would spend some time together. But there was no need to make it legally binding.

Worry about her grandfather mingled with worry for her son and herself and Fia curled up in the bed, but there was no rest to be found in sleep, the dreams racing over her in a dark, tangled rush of disturbing images. Her mother, huddled in a corner of the kitchen, trying to make herself as small as possible while her husband lost his temper. The sight of her walking away, leaving her eight-year-old daughter behind. *'If I take you, he'll come after me.'* Standing with her grandfather as they buried her father after the drunken boating accident that had taken his life, knowing that she was supposed to feel sad.

She awoke to find herself alone in the bed. A lurch of fear was followed by a brief moment of relief as she heard the sound of Luca giggling. And then she remembered that they weren't at home, but in Santo's deathtrap apartment.

Almost tripping in her haste to get to her child, she shot out of the bedroom and followed the sound, ready to drag him out of trouble.

Expecting to find an energetic Luca fearlessly scaling a cupboard or plunging his curious fingers into a piece of high-tech electrical equipment, she instead found him sitting on a chair in Santo's sleek, contemporary kitchen watching as his father deftly cut shapes out of *brioche*.

Weak with relief, Fia paused in the doorway, astonished by what she was seeing. Father or not, Santo was a stranger to Luca. A tall, powerfully built intimidating stranger who was in an undeniably dangerous mood since he'd made the unexpected discovery that he had a son. It was true that he'd helped and supported her the night before, but nothing in his demeanour had led her to believe that there was any soften-ing in his attitude.

She'd assumed that some of his anger would reveal itself in his interaction with the child and yet Luca was clearly not only comfortable, but vastly entertained and delighted with the masculine attention he was receiving along with his break-fast.

Judging from his damp hair, Santo had not long left the shower and it was obvious from his bare feet and bare chest that he'd tugged on a pair of jeans in haste, unable to finish dressing before Luca had demanded his attention. But the real change wasn't in his dress—or lack of it—it was the way he carried himself. There was no sign of the forbidding, in-timidating businessman who had called all the shots the day before. The man currently entertaining one small boy was warm and approachable, his smile indulgent as he wiped his son's buttery fingers. He looked as though he did this every day. As if this was part of their morning routine.

As she watched, Santo bent down and kissed Luca and when the child giggled, he kissed him again as if he couldn't get enough of him.

Tears sprang to her eyes and Fia leaned against the door-frame for support.

Watching them made her heart clench. Luca had never had that, had he? He'd never known a father's love. Yes, she'd surrounded him by 'family' but even she couldn't pretend that what she'd created came close to the real thing. One day Gina would move on, Ben would marry and Luca's 'family' would disband.

Yesterday she'd been so sure that marriage between her and Santo would be the wrong thing for her son. She'd seen no benefit to him in being forced to live with two people whose only connection was the child they'd made.

But of course there *was* benefit and she was staring at it right now.

If they married, Luca would have his father. Not at prear-ranged times, like single snapshots taken on a camera. But permanently.

Santo still hadn't noticed her and, as he spoke to their son in lilting Italian, Fia found that she was holding her breath. When Luca replied in the same language pride mingled with emotions she didn't even recognise.

She was normally the one who gave Luca his breakfast. It was their morning ritual. And yet here he was happily pursu-ing that ritual with his father as if the two of them had been doing it for ever.

There was a lump in her throat and the lump grew as Santo leaned forward and kissed his son again, indifferent to buttery fingers that grabbed at his hair. He blew bubbles into Luca's neck and made him giggle. He pulled faces and tickled him.

He had nieces, she remembered, so he was obviously used to children, but still—

She couldn't ever remember being kissed by her father and she'd certainly never been kissed by her grandfather. And yet here was Santo, openly demonstrative with his child.

'Mamma—' Luca saw her, wriggled off the chair and hurled himself at her, *brioche* squashed in his fist.

Across the top of his head, her gaze met Santo's.

As she scooped up her child, she swallowed down that lump that still threatened to choke her.

A quizzical gleam lit his eyes, as if he were asking himself how long she'd been standing there. And suddenly she was very conscious that she hadn't even paused to brush her hair before sprinting from the bedroom.

There was something inappropriately informal about greeting him with her hair spilling wildly over her shoulders while wearing nothing but the shirt he'd lent her. Their attire suggested an intimacy that didn't exist and she felt herself flush with mortification as his eyes slid down her body and lingered on her bare legs.

'Buongiorno.' He injected the word with familiarity. As if this was a scene they both woke up to every morning.

Even though he'd dragged on his jeans in a hurry he looked utterly spectacular. Indecently handsome and more masculine than any single member of the species had a right to look. He didn't need the handmade suits to look good, she thought numbly, her eyes tracing the smooth swell of muscle that shaped his broad shoulders and drifting to his board-flat abdomen.

'Fia?'

She was so distracted by his naked torso that she'd missed the question he'd asked her. 'Sorry?'

'I asked you which language you use when you speak to him. English or Italian?'

'English—' Thoroughly flustered, she sat Luca back down on the chair. 'My grandfather spoke to him in Italian. We thought that would be less confusing.' She braced herself for criticism of that approach but he gave a brief nod.

'Then we will do the same. You do the English. I'll do the Italian. That's what I did this morning and he seemed to understand. He's very bright.' Pride in his eyes as he looked at Luca, he rose to his feet with that easy grace guaranteed to draw the female eye. The fabric of his jeans clung to the hard length of his long legs and she saw the muscles in his back ripple as he reached into a cupboard for a mug. *She'd drawn blood*, she remembered. She'd been so driven out of her mind by him, she'd scratched the skin of that smooth, muscled back. The craving had been so intense, the pleasure so deliciously erotic that she'd dragged her nails down his flesh. Not that he'd been gentle. The recollection set her skin on fire. The whole thing had been a hot, hard, violent explosion of earthy animal instinct.

And now she was hyperaware of every move he made. Of the flex of muscle in his strong wrist as he made her coffee, of the dark hairs that shadowed his chest and then narrowed down and disappeared below the snap of his jeans. Everything about him was overtly, unapologetically male and everything about her response was overtly, unapologetically female.

He was the hottest guy she'd ever laid eyes on. Always had been. And that was what made this situation so much harder.

His gaze flicked to hers, those slumberous eyes darkening as he read her mind. Despite the presence of their child, the brief moment they shared was wholly adult.

Desperate to break the connection, Fia blurted out the first thing that came into her head. 'My phone battery has died. May I use yours to call the hospital?'

The sardonic curve of his mouth told her he knew she hadn't been thinking about phones or hospitals. And neither had he. Just being in the same room created something so intense that it was almost tangible. It crackled the air between them and snapped the atmosphere tight.

'I've already called.' He placed coffee on the table without asking her how she took it. 'Your grandfather had a good night. He's still asleep. The consultant will be at the hospital in half an hour. I've said we'll meet him there.'

We?

She watched as Luca slid off his chair and wrapped his arms around his father's legs. Santo scooped him up. 'I'm starting to understand why you were worried last night,' he drawled. 'He's extremely active.'

'But you're coping well,' she said quickly, 'so he can stay with you while I go to the hospital.' She needed respite from the unrelenting stress of being with him. Most of all she needed respite from the constant assault on her senses and the memories that kept replaying in her head. Her heart was going crazy. She was so conscious of him that she couldn't breathe properly.

He lowered Luca to the floor. 'I'm coming with you.'

'I'd rather go on my own.'

'Of course you would.' His eyes glinted with deadly mockery. 'You'd rather do everything on your own, but you're never going to learn differently if you don't practise, so you can start this morning. We'll go together. Say the word after me, Fia. *Together.*'

Fia stared at her coffee. 'Do you have milk? I like milk in my coffee. Not that I'd expect you to know that because you don't really know anything about me, do you? Just as I don't know anything about you. And that is why this is so ridiculous.' But the heat had gone out of her argument. Last night she'd been certain, now she was just confused.

'Stop trying to pick a fight. I'll win.'

She breathed, 'All right, we'll go together. But in that case I need to use a phone. I'll call Ben and ask him to pick up

Luca. He's too little to be in a place like that for more than a short time.'

The change in him was instantaneous. Any trace of humour was wiped out. It was like watching a cloud suddenly pass over the sun, darkening the land beneath. Those eyes went from burnished gold to deadly black, the threat in them unmistakable. 'You will *not* call Ben.'

'I don't want Luca at the hospital. It's exhausting for my grandfather and stressful for him.'

'I agree. Which is why I've arranged—' He broke off as they both heard a commotion at the entrance of his apartment.

'Santo?' a female voice sang out and then a beautiful dark-haired girl strode confidently into the room. Clearly familiar with the layout of the place, she kissed Santo soundly. 'You,' she purred, patting his cheek with her hand, 'are a *very* naughty boy.'

Fia sat still, frozen to the spot by the sight of this beautiful creature and the ease with which she interacted with Santo. And, to make her pain even worse, he didn't even have the gall to look embarrassed. Instead he simply unpeeled the woman, gave her a smile and kissed her on both cheeks.

'Ciao, bellissima.'

Wounded by his lack of sensitivity, Fia stood up abruptly and was about to snatch her son and leave them to it when the woman turned to look at her.

Braced for bared teeth and female jealousy, Fia found herself suddenly wrapped in a tight, effusive hug.

Apart from Luca, no one ever hugged her. The shock of it kept her rigid, but before she could work out who the woman was she'd released her and turned her attention to Luca.

First she covered her mouth with her hands as if she couldn't believe what she was seeing. Then she scooped an unsuspecting Luca up and showered him with kisses, talking in rapid Italian as she danced round the kitchen with him.

And, instead of howling, Luca seemed delighted by the attention, responding to the woman's infectious smile with gurgles of laughter.

Fia wanted to snatch her son out of the woman's arms.

Which one of Santo's many women was she?

She racked her brain to recreate all those media images of Santo she'd tried to obliterate from her mind. Santo Ferrara and a lean brunette at the opening of the Taormina Filmfest, dining out with a sleek blonde on his arm, leaving his private jet at the airport with a redhead in tow. She'd tried to blot out the female faces, not commit them to memory.

She was just about to make a taut comment when a small girl, a little older than Luca, rocketed into the room and slammed into Santo's legs.

'Up!'

'I think you mean, "up, please", but your wish is my command, of course.' His amused drawl suggesting that this was a frequent request, Santo scooped the child up. 'You need to put in some overtime on the manners here.' He glanced at the woman and his expression softened. 'Thanks for coming.'

'Anything for you.' With a cheeky smile the brunette put Luca down, dropped her bag on the chair and looked at Fia. 'I'm really sorry to hear about your grandfather. You must be worried sick, but honestly the hospital is just brilliant. And I expect Santo has them hopping around because he always puts a bomb under them. And you're not to worry about Luca. We'll keep him with us until you're ready to pick him up. I can't wait to get to know him better.'

Fia felt a flash of fury. Santo expected her to leave her son with one of his women? 'There is no way—'

'Dani is my sister, yes? Daniela Ferrara. Although technically she's no longer Ferrara since she married Raimondo.' Interrupting smoothly, Santo put the little girl down on the floor. 'This is Rosa, her daughter. Luca's cousin.'

Cousin?

Startled, Fia looked at Dani, who looked right back. 'Er… you didn't know I was Santo's sister?'

'I didn't recognise you.' Fia's voice was a croak and Dani's eyes widened in contrition.

'Oh, no! You must have thought—' Looking at her brother, she gave an exaggerated shudder. 'Nightmare. We'd kill each other in two minutes. I like to be in charge in my relationships. Talking of which, Raimondo is parking the car. We thought we'd take Luca back home with us because we have all Rosa's toys there so it's easier.' She caught Fia's anxious look and smiled. 'You're thinking you can't let him go with a stranger, I know you are because I'd be thinking the same thing in your position. But honestly, he's going to have a great time and better with us than in that vile hospital or here. Santo's apartment is a deathtrap. You two can spend as long as you need to at the hospital and then go out to dinner or something. Don't rush. Do something romantic.'

'*Cristo*, you are like a one-woman talk show. Breathe, Dani!' Santo cast his sister a look of raw exasperation. 'Give someone else the opportunity to speak! You accuse me of being controlling and then you steamroller people with words. Conversation is supposed to be a two-way thing.'

'Well, no one else is saying anything in this room!' Dani bristled and Santo ground his teeth.

'Was there an opportunity? *Accidenti!* I don't know how Raimondo puts up with you. I would strangle you within two minutes of being alone together.'

'I would have strangled you first.' Dani turned to Fia. 'Don't let him bully you. Stand up to him; it's the only way to handle Santo, especially when he does his threatening act. I used to see you sometimes on the beach but you've obviously forgotten me.'

No, she hadn't forgotten. She just hadn't recognised the

other woman and now she didn't know what to say. How much did Daniela know? What exactly had he told his family?

It should have been a horribly awkward moment but Dani clearly didn't tolerate 'awkward' in her life. She said something in Italian to her little girl, who eyed up Luca, clearly decided he looked like someone she could play with and promptly dragged him off towards Santo's living room, leaving the adults alone.

'There. See? They're friends already.' Oblivious to her brother's glowering disapproval, Dani followed them out of the room. 'I'll watch them. There is nothing you can teach me about intercepting toddler trouble.' At the doorway of the kitchen, she glanced over her shoulder. 'I'll leave you two to discuss wedding details. And Santo, it doesn't matter how rushed a wedding is, a woman still needs to look her best so you'd better take Fia shopping. Or, better still, give me your card and *I'll* take her shopping because we all know you hate it.'

Santo's expression went from irritated to dangerous. 'Your help with Luca is welcomed. Your interference in any other aspect of my life is not.'

'Just because you've done all this in the wrong order is no reason not to make it romantic,' Dani said tartly. 'A woman wants romance on her wedding day. Remember that.'

She vanished to supervise the children, leaving Fia with her face burning.

Romance?

Whatever was between them, it certainly wasn't romance. What was romantic about a man being forced to marry a woman he didn't even like?

Santo drained his coffee cup and thumped it down on the table. 'I apologise for my sister,' he breathed. 'She still hasn't learned the meaning of the word "boundary". But if she will take Luca for us today, it will make everything a lot easier.'

Nothing, absolutely nothing, would make this situation easier.

The tension between them was like a dark storm brewing in the room. She couldn't imagine ever being able to relax with him. She was wound so tight that every reaction and response was exaggerated. Her senses were heightened so that the slightest glance was all it took to set her heart pounding.

The look he sent her told her that he felt it too. 'It is good that she has taken Luca because we need to talk. Properly.'

Fia thought about Luca being hugged and kissed by his father.

Santo clearly interpreted her silence as refusal. 'You can throw as many obstacles as you like between us,' he said softly, 'and I will smash through all of them. Be sure of that. You can say no a thousand different ways and I will find a thousand different ways to tell you why you're wrong.'

'I'm not saying no.'

'Scusi?'

'I'm agreeing with you. You said that you thought marriage was the best thing for Luca, and I'm agreeing with you.' Her voice wasn't entirely steady. 'Last night I was sure that marriage wasn't in Luca's best interests but this morning…well, I saw the two of you together and…and, yes, I think it would be the right thing for Luca.' Oh, God, she'd said it. What if she were wrong?

Silence pulsed.

'So you're doing this because you think it's the right thing "for Luca"?'

'Of course. What else?'

He strode across the kitchen towards her.

Fia forced herself to stand still, expecting him to stop, but he didn't stop until he had her with her back against the wall and nowhere to go.

Jaw tight, he slammed a hand either side of her to block

her escape. She was boxed in by rock-hard muscle and testosterone and because she didn't want to look at him, she looked at his bare chest and that was a mistake too because everything about him made her think of that night. She didn't need a close-up of his physique to know how strong he was. She'd felt that strength. *Why the hell hadn't he pulled on a shirt?* The world around her seemed to fade. She forgot she was in his kitchen. She forgot about her grandfather in the hospital and the cheerful sounds of her child playing in the next room. She forgot everything.

Her world became this man.

'Look at me.' His thickened command told her that if she didn't, he'd make her and so she lifted her gaze and the look they shared unlocked something dark she'd buried deep inside herself. Something she hadn't dared examine because she was so afraid of it.

The way she felt about him.

Breathing shallow, she stared into those burnished dark eyes that changed colour according to his mood.

'This is not just about Luca and I need you to acknowledge that because I don't want some martyr in my bed.' He lowered his head, his mouth as close to hers as it was possible to be and yet not touch her. He spoke so softly that he couldn't possibly be overheard and yet each word was delivered with such force and power that she knew they'd be forever embedded in her memory. 'If we do this, then we do it properly.'

If she licked her lips now, she'd touch him. If she made that single move she'd be kissing him. And she knew how that would feel. Knew how *he'd* feel. Even after more than three years, she'd never forgotten it. 'Yes. We do it properly. We…get to know each other.'

'I already know a lot about you—'. That wicked, sensual mouth held hers hostage. 'I may not know how you like your coffee, but I know other things about you. Want me to remind you?'

'No.' She didn't need reminding. She'd forgotten nothing. Not the way he tasted nor the way he touched her. And now those memories were unlocked and she could feel herself melting—feel the heat of her own arousal spread through her body and the hard pressure of his.

His hand came up to cup her face, those same fingers that knew how to drive her wild, now firm and determined as they forced her to look at him. 'Sure? Because if this is going to work for Luca, it has to work for us.' His mouth was just a breath away from hers, the heat of him a pulsing, throbbing force. 'I have to get to know all of you, particularly the bits you're hiding. And you have to get to know all of me, *tesoro*. Everything.'

CHAPTER SIX

OVER the next few days she experienced the full might and force of the Ferrara machine. Her grandfather was moved to a private room to convalesce, his near miraculous recovery attributed to Santo's prompt intervention but also an astonishing will to live. And that will, the staff believed, came from a determination to see his granddaughter marry. And Santo fed that determination by keeping him appraised of the wedding plans—plans in which Fia had little input.

'If you have any requests then let me know,' Santo said one morning as they drove back from the hospital. 'We'll marry at the Ferrara Spa Resort, our flagship hotel. It's licensed for weddings and it's a beautiful venue, right on the beach. I'm planning on keeping it as small as possible.'

Of course he was. This wedding wasn't something to broadcast, was it?

'I'd like to invite Ben and Gina.'

He tensed slightly at the mention of Ben's name and she fully expected him to refuse, but instead he nodded. 'Yes. They are an important part of Luca's life. They should be there. I will arrange it.'

He arranged everything, or rather his team did.

It was his insistence that one of his top chefs step in to run the Beach Shack that enabled her to spend as much time with her grandfather as she needed to in those early days. And the occasional phone call to Ben was all it took to reassure her that all was well with the restaurant and that the new chef was following Santo's orders to run the place exactly as Fia ran it.

She wanted to be angry that he'd taken over, but the truth was that Santo had taken a hideous, stressful situation and made it as smooth for her as he possibly could. Because of him, her grandfather was making a good recovery, her business was safe and her child was happy.

And every time she felt wobbly about her decision, she just had to look at how he was with Luca.

'My staff have interviewed and appointed three nurses with excellent qualifications who will provide round the clock care for your grandfather when he is discharged home.' Santo negotiated the thick traffic with the ease of a native Sicilian. 'They will work on a rota so that your grandfather will never be alone.'

For years her only mode of transport had been her dusty old moped. Now each journey was made in supercharged, superaccelerated, air-conditioned luxury. 'I can't afford that level of care.'

'But I can. And I am the one paying.'

'I don't want your money. I can look after him myself. I've been running a successful business since I was eighteen.'

'Even if you were not about to marry me, that would be an unsustainable proposition. You cannot raise a child, run a business and be a full-time carer.'

'Plenty of people do just that. You may have missed the press release because it was sent to "modern man" and you don't fall into that category, but it is possible to have it all.'

'In my experience "having it all" usually includes a nervous breakdown,' Santo drawled, leaning on his horn as the driver in front stopped to let out a passenger and blocked the road. 'I want a wife, not a basket case so we'll buy in the appropriate help, which should leave you with the energy for the important parts.'

'I presume you consider the "important parts" to take place in your bedroom.'

'Funnily enough, I didn't mean that. I was talking about the energy required to care for a young child but yes, sex is going to keep you busy too. I'm a demanding guy, *angelo mia*. I have needs.' The engine growled as he accelerated past the car, shifting gears smoothly. 'And if you're going to satisfy those needs, you're going to need your sleep.'

She had a feeling he was winding her up but she didn't know him well enough to be sure.

He was ferociously bright, that she *was* sure about, but he also made no apology for being a red-blooded male.

All he'd used were words and yet the desire came in a rush, the force of it shocking her because she'd never felt this way with any other man and she didn't want to feel it about this one. Beneath all the worry and the questions, she was woman enough to wonder whether everything she remembered from that night was real or whether she'd imagined it all.

Yes, he'd been demanding, but she'd been demanding, too. In fact she couldn't even remember who had made the first move in the thick sweltering darkness of that hot summer night. He'd slaked his appetite and she'd slaked hers. He'd taken and she'd taken right back.

Because she didn't want to think about sex, she went back to something he'd said earlier. 'There is one thing you've forgotten in all this. You've forgotten to make me sign a prenuptial agreement.'

He laughed. 'We're *not* going to need one of those.'

'Don't be so sure. You're a very rich guy. Aren't you afraid I'm going to take you for every penny you have?'

'A prenuptial agreement is only necessary in the event of a divorce. I'm very traditional. I believe that marriage is for ever. Once a Ferrara wife, always a Ferrara wife. We will *not* be getting a divorce.'

'Maybe you'll want one.' She didn't understand her need to goad him but she couldn't help herself. 'Maybe you won't find being married to me particularly entertaining.'

'As long as you focus on one particular type of entertainment, we'll be fine.'

She decided he was definitely winding her up and threw him a look. 'If you're so damn horny how can you be sure marriage is going to suit you? Being trapped with one woman might drive you mad.'

'Been reading my press coverage?' He threw her an amused glance and a sexy smile that travelled right through her body. 'I never said I wasn't going to keep you busy but you can relax. You have no reason to be jealous. I intend to focus all my attention on you. *All* of it, *tesoro*.' His husky voice teased her nerve-endings. Or maybe it was the words again. The way he managed to inject each phrase with lethal promise. Under that veneer of smooth control she sensed darker emotions that simmered beneath the surface he presented to the world. From the rocky base of her own family, she'd watched him grow from boy to man. She understood the volatility that was so much a part of his nature, but she'd also seen the drive. Unobserved, she'd watched as he'd learned to windsurf and to sail. She'd admired the sheer determination that never allowed him to give up on anything until it was mastered. And then there had been the women. Golden-haired girls who flocked to the beach in the hope of attracting the attention of one of the Ferrara brothers.

It was no wonder he was sure of himself, she thought numbly. No one had ever said no to him. No one had ever challenged his supremacy. And suddenly she couldn't help herself.

'Maybe *you* won't be enough for *me*,' she said calmly, deciding to play him at his own game. 'I have needs too. Needs every bit as powerful as yours. Maybe you won't be able to satisfy me.'

Dark eyebrows rose, but the faint gleam in his eyes suggested he appreciated the humour. 'You think not?'

'No. I don't see why men always think they have the monopoly on sexual needs. I'm just saying that perhaps I'll be the one looking elsewhere.'

He stopped the car so suddenly that the seat belt locked.

Oblivious to the cacophony of horns sounding behind them, he turned to face her and her heart raced away in a crazy rhythm under that glittering gaze because the humour was gone.

'I didn't mean it,' she muttered. She realised she'd been stupid to goad him in that way. 'You were winding me up and I was doing the same. For goodness' sake, Santo—my father was unfaithful to my mother for the whole of their marriage, do you really think I'd do that?'

He inhaled slowly. 'Not a good joke.'

'No, but—' she hesitated '—since this conversation has turned serious—I'm well aware that you're marrying me just because of Luca so we're not exactly glued together by love, are we? I'm not a meek, obedient girl who is going to sit in the corner while you go off with other women. What happens if you do fall in love?'

He stared at her for a long moment and then turned his attention back to the road and eased back into the horrendous traffic. 'I'd be bored silly in five minutes with meek and obedient. I don't want you to sit in a corner. As my wife you will inevitably have a high profile. And whatever happened in the past, I respect you as the mother of my child and that is enough to glue us together. And as for your father—' his voice hardened '—his behaviour was dishonourable and beneath contempt. I would never behave in such a way towards the mother of my children. You have no need to worry. And no need to be jealous.'

Humiliated that she'd revealed so much, she turned her head and looked out of the window but she was oblivious to everything except her own emotions. She realised that she didn't even know where they were. She'd been so wrapped up in her emotions she hadn't been watching the route. 'I'm not jealous.'

'Yes, you are. You're worried I'm going to cheat on you and I don't mind that because it proves you're committed—' He leaned on his horn and overtook a driver who he obviously considered to be going too slowly. 'If you'd told me to go ahead and have an affair, I would have been worried. You feel strong emotions and I'm comfortable with strong emotions. I just need to persuade you to express them. From now on "hiding in the boathouse" is banned. And I use that term figuratively as well as literally.'

She hadn't been back to the boathouse for years. Once, it had been her favourite hiding place, her sanctuary, but she hadn't been back there since that night.

Santo drove into the courtyard of a beautiful palazzo and Fia glanced around her in surprise.

'Where are we?'

'My brother Cristiano's town house. You're choosing your wedding dress. Dani is here and also Cristiano's wife, Laurel. You'll like her. She is calmer than Dani so hopefully she'll add some sense to the proceedings.'

'They separated—' she frowned, trying to remember '—I read something in the paper.'

'But now they are back together and stronger than ever. They have a daughter, Elena, who is the same age as Dani's Rosa, and an older daughter, Chiara, who they adopted a year ago.' He switched off the engine. 'So you see, Luca's family is expanding by the minute.'

'I read that they were getting a divorce.'

'Not any more.' He gave a gentle smile and released her seat belt. 'As I said, *angelo mia,* once a Ferrara wife, always a Ferrara wife. Remember that.'

She got through the wedding ceremony by telling herself that she was marrying for love. Not love for Santo, but love for her son. And any doubts she might have had were swept away by the sight of Luca being welcomed into the big, noisy Ferrara family. He thrived on the attention, adored playing with his cousins and wouldn't let his father out of his sight. And Fia couldn't help but warm to Santo's mother, who embraced her tightly as she welcomed her to the family. They never held anything back, she thought. They didn't ration love. They weren't afraid that too much was a bad thing.

The media, tired of the endless gloom of economic disaster, greedily devoured a happy story. Thanks to the few choice details fed to them by the Ferrara publicity machine, they'd pieced together a romantic tale that bore no resemblance to reality. According to the press, their relationship had been conducted in secret because of the long-standing feud between their families, but now it was out in the open and the headlines read 'Love conquers all'.

But perhaps the press were most charmed by the sight of her grandfather and Cristiano Ferrara shaking hands and talking together at length, finally putting an end to hostilities.

'I'm worried this is all too much for you, *Nonno.*' The tension a constant knot in her stomach, Fia sat down on the chair next to her grandfather. 'You should still be convalescing.'

'Don't fuss. Ferrara has half the hospital standing guard,' her grandfather grumbled. 'What can happen?'

But she could tell he was impressed by the care and attention Santo had paid to him and if her insides hadn't been churning so alarmingly at the thought of what was coming, she would have been grateful, too. As it was, she stole a glance at the handsome man who was now her husband and felt a flicker of trepidation. It was all very well for him to say that marriage was for ever but, apart from the moment they'd exchanged vows, he hadn't looked at her. Not once. It was as if he were trying to postpone the moment he had to confront reality. What would happen when the guests finally left and they were alone? Would there be stilted conversation? Would he suggest an early night?

Her grandfather gave a rare smile. 'Look at Luca. Now *that's* how a boy should play.'

Fia looked and saw her son shrieking with laughter as his father held him upside down by his ankles. She felt a lurch of anxiety.

'I hope he doesn't drop him on the terrace.'

Her grandfather gave her an impatient look. 'You fuss him to death.'

Did she fuss him to death? She'd tried so hard to make sure Luca knew he was loved. Had she overdone that?

'I just want him to be happy.'

'And what about you? Are you happy?' It was the first time her grandfather had ever asked her that question and she didn't know how to answer.

She should have been happy that Luca now had his father in his life and that the long-running feud between their two families had finally been put to rest.

But how happy could a marriage be when the only love involved was for a child?

Her father had made no secret of his resentment towards his children. He'd married because of pressure from his father—her grandfather—and four lives had been damaged as a result of his innate selfishness.

But Santo was nothing like her father, she reasoned. It was obvious that he felt nothing but unconditional love for his son and already Luca was being enveloped in the warm, protective blanket of the Ferrara family.

'I'm giving him the land as a wedding gift.' Her grandfather scowled at her. 'Satisfied?'

She gave a weak smile. 'Yes. Thank you.'

He hesitated and then squeezed her hand in an almost unprecedented show of affection. 'You did the right thing. Eventually.'

The right thing for Luca, yes. But for her?

She was less convinced.

Eventually the guests started to drift away. Her grandfather, tired but less grumpy than she'd seen him in a long time, was ushered away by concerned health staff and only a few close family remained.

Feeling alone in the crowd of Ferraras, Fia paced restlessly to the far side of the terrace where they had gathered to 'celebrate'.

'Here—' Dani thrust a glass of champagne into her hand '—you look as though you need it. Welcome to the family. You look stunning. That dress is perfect, if I say so myself.' She clinked her glass against Fia's. 'To your future, which is going to be good, despite what you're thinking right now this minute.'

Fia wondered how she knew. She wasn't used to confiding in people. On the other hand, she was grateful to Dani for at least making an effort to be friendly. 'Am I that easy to read?'

'Yes.' Dani stretched out a hand and brushed a strand of hair from Fia's shoulder. 'I know that you and Santo have your problems; I'm not fooled by this story he's spinning for the world. But it's going to be fine now you're married. You'll work it out. There's something strong between you. I sensed it that morning I arrived to help with Luca. You could barely keep your hands off each other.'

That was just sexual chemistry and Fia knew you couldn't build a marriage on that. 'He's angry with me.'

'He's Santo,' Dani said simply. 'He feels deeply. About everything, but most of all family. Cristiano is the same. But now you *are* family.'

'But he didn't really want to marry me.' The words came out in a rush. 'I'm irrelevant.'

'Irrelevant?' Dani looked at her for a long time and then smiled. 'Let me tell you something about my brother. Whatever you may have heard, he is very, *very* picky when it comes to women and he believes that marriage is for ever. He would not have married you if he didn't think the two of you could make a go of it.'

'I don't think he's thought about us at all. This is about Luca.'

'But you made Luca together,' Dani said gently, 'so there must have been something. And you're certainly not irrelevant. He's spent the whole evening trying not to look at you.'

'You noticed that?' Her humiliation deepened but Dani smiled.

'It's a good sign. I have a suspicion my very confident brother is feeling confused for the first time in his life. That *has* to be a good thing.'

'I took it as a sign that he's indifferent.'

'I don't know what he feels but it's not indifference.'

Fia had no chance to question her further because Dani was immediately dragged away to speak to a bunch of cousins and Fia was left alone again. She was now married to one of the wealthiest men in Italy, but she longed to be back at the Beach Shack, clearing up after evening service, with the prospect of an early-morning dip in the sea with her son.

It had been agreed that Luca would stay with Dani and her family for the night and the thought of being without him brought a lump to her throat. Suddenly she wanted to scoop up her son and run straight back into her old life where her emotions and feelings had been a steady, predictable thing. Instead she had to hug him goodbye and watch as he left with his new family. Was it selfish to wish he were just a little anxious about leaving her? Was it wrong of her to wish he'd clung just a little longer instead of smiling with excitement at the prospect of spending more time with his cousins? Was it cowardly to wish she had him here, because he formed the only effective barrier between herself and Santo?

'He'll be fine. Don't worry about him. Dani may seem scatty but she's a devoted mother.' Santo was by her side. Santo, who was now her husband, for richer, for poorer. And it was definitely richer, she thought numbly. Even knowing how wealthy the Ferrara family were, she was still stunned by the sheer luxury of her new life. This was their flagship hotel and their corporate headquarters and at the far side of the private beach was the Aphrodite Villa, the jewel in the Ferrara corporate crown. Occasionally the family rented it to rock stars and royalty, but for the next twenty-four hours it belonged to them and the thought of being alone with Santo in a place designed for lovers made her feel something close to panic.

Over the past week she'd been so busy taking care of Luca, shuttling backwards and forward to the hospital to be with her grandfather, she'd managed not to face up to the reality of their wedding night. But now—

Suddenly she longed for those distractions that had kept her from thinking about this moment. The moment she'd be on her own with Santo.

'He didn't need to be sent away.' She kept her eyes fixed on the distance, determined not to look at him. If he could ignore her, she would ignore him back. 'It isn't as if he's intruding on a romantic interlude. It's crazy to turn this into something it's not.'

Her observation was met with silence.

Unnerved by that silence, she glanced briefly at him and collided with night-black eyes that glittered bright with intent.

'You don't think he'd be intruding?' He slid his hand behind her head and brought her face close to his. 'You want him here while we finally let this thing between us go free? Is that what you want?' His voice was thickened with raw lust. 'Because I, for one, have no intention of holding back. I've been doing that for long enough and it's driving me insane.'

Shocked, Fia stared into those eyes. She could see the blaze of hunger. Feel the hard bite of his fingers as he buried them in her hair. And everything he felt, she felt too. How could she not? The chemistry was so powerful that she felt it shoot right through her. She burned up and melted. It might have ended right there on the terrace had not someone cleared their throat right next to them.

This time it was Cristiano, Santo's older brother. Unlike Dani, he'd been cool with her and Fia suspected he wasn't going to be so easily won over as his romantic sister.

Brotherly love, she thought numbly.

She'd never had that. Her brother had been selfish and irresponsible and any warmth in their relationship had existed only in her mind. Unlike the Ferraras, where warmth surrounded the family like a protective forcefield.

With visible reluctance, Santo let his hand drop from her neck. 'Back in a minute.' Relaxed and unflustered, he strolled away with his brother and Fia took advantage of the distraction to make an exit. She had no intention of waiting. The atmosphere was suffocating and anyway, what was he planning? A romantic walk on the sand? Hardly.

Solar-powered lights lit the path to the beach and she walked quickly, blotting out the thought that this place was perfect for a lovers' stroll. The setting sun sent a ruby glow over the darkening horizon and in the background she heard the rhythmic chirruping of cicadas and the soft swish of the sea on the sand.

It should have been an idyllic setting but the perfection jarred against the reality.

It felt as inappropriate as the cream silk wedding dress chosen by Dani.

She should have worn red, she thought. Red for danger.

She approached the villa, was momentarily checked by the sheer beauty of the infinity pool and then stopped dead at the sight that greeted her. It was obvious that the place had been lovingly prepared for a night of romance. The doors were open to the beach. Chilled champagne waited by the bed, candles flickered on every surface and rose petals had been scattered on the floor leading to the luxurious bedroom.

She could have coped with the champagne and the candles.

It was the sight of those rose petals that made her throat close.

Rose petals said romance, and that wasn't what was going on here.

Their relationship was *not* about romance.

Emotions that had been building since Santo had first strode into her kitchen exploded. Trying to destroy the atmosphere created by the candles, she flicked on harsh overhead lights and started to open doors, looking for a broom— looking for something that would help her remove that romantic symbol from the floor. When she failed to find anything remotely like cleaning equipment she dropped to her knees and started to scoop the petals up by hand, sweeping them into a pile by the bed.

'What the hell are you doing?' An incredulous male voice came from the doorway but Fia didn't even look up. She didn't dare look up in case everything she was feeling spilled over.

'What does it look like I'm doing? I'm clearing up the evidence of someone's warped sense of humour.' The mound was growing but before she could add any more she was lifted off her knees and planted on her feet.

'What's warped about it?'

'It's a mockery,' she croaked. 'Someone is being intentionally cruel. Making fun of our relationship.'

Dark brows locked together in an uncomprehending frown. '*I* gave the instruction to prepare it the way we do for honeymoons and romantic breaks. I just married you. Short though it may be, this is our honeymoon. There are certain expectations. I've projected this as a romance because I don't want any rumours that will hurt our son.'

So even the rose petals by the bed were for Luca. All of it was for Luca.

'But he's not here now, is he? And neither are the journalists. So we can lose the rose petals.' Her teeth were chattering and he made an impatient sound and his fingers tightened on her shoulders.

'What is the significance of a few rose petals?'

'Precisely! They have no significance! They have no place in our relationship, and if you can't see that—' She tugged herself away from him. 'I think you are the most insensitive man I've ever met. I've gone along with this whole white wedding charade although I would have been quite happy just to have kept it small—'

'That was small.'

Fia wasn't listening. 'I've bitten my tongue when the press have gone on about Romeo and Juliet which, by the way, isn't actually the best analogy given that both of them die at the end, I said my vows and I gave you my son. I did all that not because I have feelings for you but because I have feelings for *him* and I can see that already he loves you! I'm prepared to do all that for him and I'm prepared to be nice Mommy when we're all together but when we're alone—that's different.' Suddenly she felt exhausted and she pressed her fingers to her forehead, struggling to contain emotion that felt too big for her body. 'Do you know what? I actually respected you for not once pretending this was anything other than a marriage of convenience, mostly *your* convenience, by the way. But nowhere in our discussions have we ever pretended that what we share is about…about…' her breathing stuttered '…rose petals.'

'*Cristo*, will you stop obsessing about rose petals?'

'I just don't need rose petals in my life, OK?' She was right on the edge and the thought of losing it horrified her. 'It doesn't matter how many rose petals you arrange to have strewn on the floor, our marriage is still a sham. And now I'm going to bed. And if you have any sensitivity you'll sleep on the sofa.'

'I have it on good authority I'm an insensitive bastard, so I guess that clears up any questions over where I'll be sleeping,' he drawled. 'And don't even think about making a run for it because I'll just drag you back. Look at me.'

She looked, and if breathing had seemed hard before it was doubly hard now. As she looked into those dark sexy eyes a part of her she'd buried sprang to life. She was used to controlling her feelings. She'd learned the skill as a child. Only once in her life had she truly let herself go, and it had been with this man. That night in the darkness, the night they'd made Luca, it had been all about touch and taste, soft sounds and a wild, maddening desire. It had unnerved her then. And it unnerved her now.

Because she'd put on the lights, there was no missing the purposeful glitter in his eyes or his obvious arousal. And there was no disguising the instant response of her own body.

It had been brewing, of course, since that night he'd walked into her restaurant, but they'd both held it in check.

Now, there was nothing to snap that frighteningly powerful connection. It wasn't about candles or rose petals, but an elemental force that was stronger than both of them.

He stood absolutely still and the stillness simply raised the tension because she knew now how this was going to end.

They moved at the same time, coming together with a violence that came close to desperation. His hands cupped her face as he kissed her hard. Her hands were on the front of his shirt, ripping. And then her fingers were on his flesh and he groaned against her mouth and grabbed the hem of her dress and yanked it upwards. They stopped kissing just long enough for him to strip it over her head and then his mouth crushed hers again, his hands buried in the thickness of her hair, his powerful body pressed hard against hers as the two of them staggered backwards into the wall. Still they kissed, his tongue hot in her mouth, her hands fumbling frantically with the zip of his trousers. She yanked it down and closed her hand over the thickness of him. He gave a savage groan, his hands bold and sure as he stripped her naked.

Desire was an elemental savage rush of fire. It poured through her veins, heated her skin and weakened her limbs. It blasted all thought from her head until her most basic instincts were screaming. She was naked in front of him but she didn't even care. Her only thought was that now he could get on and do what they both needed him to do.

And he did.

His mouth found the pulse at the base of her throat and her head fell back, the excitement almost excruciating.

'*Cristo*, I want you—' His hand was between her legs and his skilled fingers slid into her, exploring her so intimately that she sobbed his name on each ragged breath.

'Please—'

'Yes—' Without hesitating, he lifted her so that she was forced to wrap her thighs around him and then he was kissing her again, his mouth feasting on hers as they yielded to the madness.

Her hands were on his bare shoulders and she felt the rippling power of his body and the strength of him as he positioned her. Like this she was helpless, but she didn't care. She was wild with the feelings they unleashed together, utterly lost in the mind-blowing excitement of his touch. He kissed her as if this moment would never, ever come again, as if the crazy collision of their mouths was the breath of life.

They dispensed with foreplay, the wild urgency of it stampeding over thoughts of taking it slow. There was no slow. Just hard, fast and desperate.

His fingers dug into her thighs and she felt the smooth tip of his penis against her and then he was inside her, hot, hard and all male. She cried out and arched, taking him deep, her body yielding to the demands of his. And he demanded everything, took everything, until her orgasm came screaming down on her and took him with her, soft, sensitive tissue clamping down on each erotic juddering thrust until the experience became one wild, mad rush of exquisite pleasure.

Fia clung to him, eyes closed, struggling for breath.

He supported her with one arm while he planted his other hand on the wall behind her in an attempt to steady himself. Muttering something in Italian, he rested his forehead on his arm and struggled for breath.

'*Madre de Dio*, that wasn't how I planned it.' He lifted his head and looked at her, those impossibly sexy eyes darkened to near black. 'Did I hurt you? You fell against the wall—'

'Don't remember that.' She felt dazed. Weak. 'I'm all in one piece.'

Except for her heart. Did that count?

But she wasn't going to think about that now. Didn't have time to think of it because he was lowering her to the floor and the moment he released her, her knees buckled. He caught her easily and dragged her against him, but that meant that they were touching again and what began as support quickly moved into seduction. They couldn't help themselves. He buried his mouth in her neck. She slid her arms around his shoulders and pressed closer. Even after that explosive climax he was still hard and she gave a soft gasp as she felt the heaviness of his erection brush against her.

'Santo—'

'You're driving me crazy—' He slid a hand behind her neck and brought his mouth down to hers. Kissed her with raw hunger. Then his other hand slid between her thighs and she stumbled against him.

'The bed—'

'Too far—' His mouth devouring hers, he tipped her off her feet, down onto the floor.

She was dimly aware of her neat pile of rose petals scattering and then he rolled onto his back so that she was the one straddling him. Strands of her hair brushed his chest and she leaned forward to kiss him, unwilling to relinquish that pleasure even for a moment. His hands sank into her hair and he crushed her mouth with his. His tongue played with hers. Teased. Tormented. Her hands grew bold and greedy, tracing his flat, muscled abdomen and moving lower to close around the thickness of his shaft. If he needed recovery time then there was no sign of it and when his hands locked on her hips and he lifted her onto him, she paused for a moment, teasing him and herself by delaying the moment. She felt the smooth probing heat of him against her and he watched her through eyes that glittered dark with barely restrained desire. There was something about that sexy, smouldering look that snapped her control and she moved her hips gracefully and took him deep.

'Cristo—' His jaw tightened and the muscles in his shoulders bulged as he drove himself into her. The power should have been hers but she felt the hard throb of him inside her and the bite of his fingers on her thighs and realised that all the power still lay with him. He controlled her. He controlled every second of the whole erotic experience and this time when her senses exploded she collapsed onto his chest and felt his arms come round her tightly.

They lay for a moment and then he winced.

'*Cristo*, this is uncomfortable. We should move.'

She didn't think she was capable of moving but he slowly eased himself onto one elbow and then frowned down at her.

'You're bleeding!'

She glanced down at her arm. 'It's a rose petal. They're stuck to you, too.'

He shifted her gently away from him and sat up, removing rose petals with an impatient hand. 'Why are rose petals considered romantic?'

'They just are—in certain circumstances.' But not these, of course. The petals had been part of the image he wanted to create.

But how could she be angry with him about that? He'd been thinking about their son. And she didn't want Luca to be the subject of gossip and speculation any more than he did.

He sprang to his feet, lean and lithe, his body at the peak of physical fitness. 'Intrigued though I am at the prospect of picking rose petals from your body all night, I think the shower might be quicker.' Taking her hand, he pulled her to her feet and drew her across the bedroom into the wetroom.

He was completely unselfconscious and relaxed as he prowled into the shower and hit a button on the wall.

Fia was still staring at the muscular perfection of his lean, bronzed back when he turned.

'Keep looking at me like that and we're not going to make it to the bed any time in the next two days,' he warned, hauling her against him and burying his hands in her hair.

Steaming jets of water covered her and she gasped as the water sluiced over her hair, her face, mingling with the heat of his kiss.

Her body was slick and damp against his.

He washed the rose petals away and she did the same with him.

Hands stroked. Mouths fused. Senses flared.

He pressed her back against the tiled wall of the shower out of the direct jets of the water and slowly kissed his way down her body. The skilled flick of his tongue across her nipples made her arch into him and he clasped her writhing hips in his hands and anchored her as he kissed his way down her body. He didn't speak and neither did she. The only sounds were the hiss of the water and her soft gasps as he boldly took every liberty he wanted to take, first with his fingers and then with his mouth. It felt too intimate, made her feel too vulnerable, and she closed her hands in his hair, intending to stop him, but then he used his tongue, teasing and tormenting until she was engulfed by a dark, erotic pleasure that threatened to overwhelm her. She wanted him to stop and carry on at the same time. She ached with wanting him and when she felt the knowing slide of his fingers deep inside her she sobbed his name and felt her body race towards completion.

'Please—' Desperate, she moved her hips and he rose to his feet, lifted her thigh to give himself access and drove himself deep into her quivering, excited body. He was hot, hard and unapologetically male, each skilful thrust so intensely arousing that she cried out and dug her fingers into his warm, naked shoulders.

She felt him throb inside her, felt him drive them both higher and higher with long, sure strokes until pleasure exploded and her muscles clenched around him, the pulsing contractions of her body propelling him to the same peak of sexual excitement.

Sated, Fia dropped her head to his damp, sleek shoulder, stunned by a pleasure she'd never known before. He pushed her wet hair away from her face, stroked her cheek with a gentle hand and muttered something in Italian that she didn't catch.

Just in that moment she felt closer to him than she ever had.

Maybe, she thought numbly, maybe it would be all right. That degree of sexual intimacy wasn't possible without some degree of feeling, was it? Maybe, if the sex was this good, the rest of it would eventually be good too.

The gentle touch of his fingers on her face made her insides melt in an entirely different way. She softened. That frozen part of herself that prevented her from allowing herself to be close to anyone thawed slightly. Feeling incredibly vulnerable, she lifted her head to look at him. She didn't know what to say, but presumably he did because if there was one thing Santo Ferrara was never short of it was smooth words. He used them in business to command and persuade and yes, he used them with women. He would know exactly the right thing to say to capture the moment.

Supporting her with one arm, he leaned across and killed the jet on the shower.

The hiss of water was silenced.

Fia held her breath and waited. She felt as if she was poised on the brink of something life-changing. As if whatever he said now would shift the direction of their relationship.

'Bed,' he said huskily, his lashes darkened and damp with water. 'This time we're going to make it to the bed, *tesoro*.'

This time we're going to make it to the bed.

Her fragile hope and expectations shattered, Fia paled. 'That's all you can say?'

Dark eyebrows rose in lazy appraisal. 'I was thinking of your comfort,' he drawled. 'So far we've had wall sex, floor sex and shower sex. I was thinking bed sex might be a progression but if you want to try something else I'm up for it. You are utterly incredible.'

'You—' Fia was so upset that she couldn't finish her sentence.

Plunged from hope into the depths of despair in the space of minutes, *furious* with herself for being so gullible as to think even for a second that he might have feelings for her, she lost her cool.

'I hate you, do you know that? Right now, this moment, Santo Ferrara, I really, *really* hate you.' But even as she said the words, she knew they weren't true. It was the very fact that they weren't true that made her so upset. She was completely confused about her feelings. She barely knew him and yet she'd allowed him to—

Fia closed her eyes, embarrassed, excited, humiliated, vulnerable—all of it. The thought of how close she'd come to revealing her feelings and making a monumental fool of herself was a dizzying experience.

His eyes were suddenly wary. 'Very intense sex can make women very emotional.'

'It's not the sex that's making me emotional, it's *you*! You're a heartless, cold hearted, arrogant…s…s…'

'—sex god?'

'*Slime ball!*' Her heart was pounding and her whole body was shaking. She sucked in deep breaths, trying to calm herself down and she might have succeeded had he not given a dismissive shrug of those wide shoulders.

'I was joking,' he said flatly, 'but suddenly you're very serious. The sexual chemistry between us is off the scale and you're obviously unsettled by that. Don't be. Instead, be grateful that at least one part of our relationship is a spectacular success. It gives us something to build on. Sex is important to me and we're clearly not going to have any problems in the bedroom. Or the bathroom. Or the floor—' His lazy humour was the final straw.

'You think not? I've got news for you—we're going to have *big* problems. Sex is just sex! You can't build on it. Especially not the type of Olympic sex you go in for. With you it's all about performance! That's not emotional, it's just physical.'

'"Just physical" has had you panting and begging for the past three hours.' Reaching past her, he grabbed a towel. 'If it was an Olympic performance you were looking for then between us I'd say we produced a gold for the team.'

'Get away from me.' She planted her hands on his bronzed chest and pushed, but he stood with his legs braced, all rock-solid muscle and glorious male nakedness. 'I don't want wall sex, floor sex or bed sex. I don't want any sex! In fact I never want you to touch me again!' She pushed past him and grabbed her own towel from the heated cabinet, noticing that the rose petals had been turned to mush by the water from the shower.

Finally, she thought wildly, something that was truly symbolic of their relationship.

Wrecked, ruined and a total mess.

CHAPTER SEVEN

'Mamma!'

Unnoticed by all concerned, Santo watched as Luca wriggled his way out of Dani's hold and sprinted across the sand to Fia. She scooped him up and hugged him tightly, her smile illuminating her whole face as she lifted him and swung him round.

'Oh, I *missed* you so much! Have you been good?'

Observing that outpouring of love and affection, Santo ground his teeth. Only an hour earlier he'd sat across from her as she'd eaten her breakfast in frozen silence. Not once had she looked at him. Any attempt on his part to engage her in conversation had resulted in monosyllabic answers.

Unable to understand how she could be upset after a night of spectacular sex, Santo's mood had grown darker with each passing minute.

Clearly the night had fallen seriously short of her romantic expectations, but what had she been expecting? He wasn't such a hypocrite as to pretend that their marriage was a great love match. That was just the story he'd given to the press to lure them away from the truth and ensure that Luca was protected from gossip. Granted the whole rose petal thing hadn't been one of his better ideas, but he'd taken her mind off them fast enough. The sex had been nothing short of mind-blowing. How could utterly mind-blowing sex have such a negative impact? Surely she should have been delighted that they were so compatible? He'd felt energized and optimistic that his hastily arranged marriage might prove to be more satisfactory than he'd ever imagined. He'd been dragged kicking and screaming into that state by his principles and his overwhelming love for his son. If his wife ended up being a hot fantasy in bed then that was a bonus.

His thoughts interrupted by the delicious sound of Luca's giggles, he turned his head to search for the cause of such hilarity and saw the two of them engaged in a tickling match that had both of them rolling on the sand. Luca tickled Fia's neck clumsily and she produced the expected response, squealing with laughter and pretending to wriggle free of him, a reaction that earned her more giggles. Santo watched that tangle of golden limbs with mixed feelings. Whatever he thought of her behaviour, she loved their son, there was no doubt about that. And Luca brought out a side of her he'd never seen before.

She was a different woman. Warm, approachable and open as she shared all of herself with her child.

Their enjoyment of each other was infectious and, without even realising what he was doing, he strode forward to join them, leaning down to join in the tickle. His son chortled and twisted and Santo's hand brushed against the side of Fia's breast.

Instantly the warmth faded from her eyes and she sprang to her feet, her expression shifting from happy to hostile in the blink of an eye. 'I didn't see you arrive. I thought you were on the phone.'

The immediate change in her stoked his temper. Luca had stopped giggling and was staring between them, confused. Acting on instinct, Santo scooped the child into his arms and then leaned forward to deliver a slow, lingering kiss to Fia's soft mouth. Heat shot through him but he banked down his own needs and kept the kiss sweet and not sexual.

When he lifted his head, her cheeks were pink and her eyes every bit as confused as their son's had been.

Something flickered there, something he couldn't quite identify.

'Never,' he said softly, 'send me that angry look in front of our child again.'

'Mamma,' Luca said happily and Santo smiled at him even though he could feel the hot rays of fury burning from Fia.

'Sì, she is your mamma.' *And she is very angry with me.* 'And now it is time we went home.'

That announcement was greeted with the same enthusiasm as an imminent storm warning.

She extracted herself from his hold and took a step backwards. 'I'm not going back to your apartment. I'm going to my restaurant today. And Luca is coming with me.'

'I agree.' Santo put Luca down on the sand. 'You need to get back to your business, and so do I. And Luca clearly has a good relationship with Gina so I'm happy for her to provide additional care while you are working. That arrangement can stay.'

'You're happy—' The outrage in her response died as he covered her lips with his fingers.

'Later,' he purred softly, 'you can thank me for preventing you from saying what you wanted to say in front of our child. Your animosity is unsettling him, *tesoro,* so from now on you will moderate your emotions unless we are alone together. That was your rule, by the way. Console yourself with the knowledge that I'm more than happy to fight you on whatever level you wish, on whichever surface you prefer once he is in bed.' Her mouth was warm against his fingers. He wanted to dip his finger inside, then his tongue, and then—

Her eyes darkened. He saw her throat move as she swallowed. Then her gaze slid to Luca, who was watching both of them closely. 'Your apartment is not a suitable place to raise an active toddler. Don't eat that, *chicco*—' Her tone altering from cool to caring, she reached down and removed the sand from Luca's fist before scooping him up protectively.

'I happen to agree with you, which is why we will not be using the apartment.'

'You said we were going home.'

'I have five homes.' Santo wondered how he could still want her so badly after a night of cataclysmic sex. 'I agree that the apartment isn't suitable for our immediate needs so I'm moving us all into our house on the beach.'

'Your childhood home?'

'The position is perfect and the structure sound. I've been renovating it for the past six months and, with a few overnight adjustments, it's perfect for a family. It has many useful features which I know will appeal to you—' he paused '—including a boathouse.'

He'd expected her to be delighted. She'd spent half her childhood hiding out there, hadn't she? She obviously liked it.

But there was no sign of the gratitude he'd been expecting. Instead her cheeks lost the last of their colour. She seemed about to speak, but then clamped her mouth shut and stared over the bay, struggling for control.

When she finally spoke, she was perfectly composed but she didn't look at him. 'We'll live wherever you want us to live, of course.'

The implication being that she would be going under sufferance.

Having expected gratitude, Santo felt a rush of frustration. He'd grown up in a family that always said what they thought. Dani said what she thought so often he frequently wanted to throttle her. Family gatherings were noisy. Everyone had an opinion and didn't hesitate to express it, usually at high volume and invariably simultaneously. He wasn't used to having to read a female mind. 'I thought you'd be pleased,' he said tightly. 'Living there will allow you to continue to run your business, visit your grandfather and still sleep in my bed.' That comment brought the colour back into her cheeks but still she didn't look at him.

Conscious of Luca, Santo bit back the comment that tasted like acid on his tongue. 'We'll be leaving in twenty minutes. Be ready.'

Confused and unsettled, Fia threw herself back into her work. And if the memory of that tender kiss lingered, she tried to eradicate it by reminding herself that it had been for the benefit of her son. There was no tenderness in what she and Santo shared. There was heat—plenty of heat. It was physical. Nothing more.

Having tried to diminish it in her mind, it was doubly frustrating that she kept thinking about it. Relieved to have something to distract her, she didn't know whether to be pleased or disappointed to discover that the Beach Shack had flourished in her absence.

'That chef Ferrara sent over here was good. He kept the menus the same, Boss.' Ben put a basket of glossy purple aubergines down on the floor. 'These look good. We put *pasta con funghi e melanzane* on the lunch menu. Are you happy with that?'

'Yes.' It felt good to throw herself back into her job and frustrating to discover that work didn't provide the distraction she needed. It didn't matter what she did, her brain kept returning to the moment the two of them had slammed into the wall, so desperate for each other that they'd thought of nothing but the need to slake their mutual lust. For years she'd longed for an experience powerful enough to overshadow the memory of the night she'd got pregnant with Luca, and now she had it tenfold.

'Er…is something wrong?' Ben gave her a nudge. 'Because you don't look as if you're concentrating and that's a dangerous way to be around a naked flame. You might burn yourself.'

It was a perfect description of how she felt after the previous night. As if she'd been scorched by a naked flame. Her entire body was still smouldering from the heat they'd produced together. Fia squeezed her eyes shut for a moment, trying to blot out the vision of smooth, powerful shoulders encasing her as he drove them both hard towards a shattering climax.

'Boss?' Ben's voice intruded on the erotic vision. 'Er… Fia?'

She gulped and snapped herself back to the present. 'What?'

'You look…distracted.'

'I'm fine,' she croaked. 'I just want to get on with the job. Right?'

Ben looked at her oddly. 'Right.'

'I'm just a bit tired. I need to concentrate, that's all.' She stared at the basket of glossy aubergines and for a moment she couldn't remember what she was supposed to do with them. All she could think about was the sensual curve of Santo's mouth as he bent his head to kiss her, of the skill of his fingers and the way he—

Furious with herself, she muttered something rude in Italian under her breath and Ben wisely scooped up the meals she'd plated up and retreated to the safety of the restaurant.

Gina was less sensitive. Being a typical girl, she wanted details. 'I read that article that said the two of you had been secretly in love since you were young—' she sighed '—that's so romantic.'

No, Fia thought grimly, frying aubergine slices until they were brown and softened. It was PR on his part, but to tell the truth would be to subject Luca to gossip so she kept silent and went along with the 'long lost love' scenario that the whole country seemed to find so heart-warming.

Only she knew that the truth was very different.

Santo had married her not because he had feelings for her, but because he wanted their son. The irony didn't escape her. She was the envy of millions of women. She'd married a superrich, supersuccessful, super-sexy man. She'd married a Ferrara.

Her first glimpse of her new home had left her reeling. She wasn't used to living in such luxury. Santo's modifications had made the most of the villa's enviable position right on the bay. Acres of glass gave it a contemporary feel, while making the most of the spectacular views of the bay and the nature reserve that pressed up against their land. No one could fail to fall in love with the house, but Fia's favourite room was the large, airy kitchen. If she'd designed it herself, this was what she would have chosen. It wasn't just a room to cook in, it was a room to live in—the heart of the home, with glass doors opening onto a terrace bordered on one side by a fruit orchard, so that picking a fresh orange for breakfast meant simply stepping outdoors and pulling one from one of the many trees. It was a place for family celebrations, for cosy breakfasts and intimate dinners. It was perfect.

She took Luca back to the villa late that afternoon, gave him tea in the beautiful kitchen and allowed him to explore. His discovery of what was clearly intended to be his bedroom drew gasps of delight and excitement.

'Boat!' He clambered onto his new bed, built in the shape of a boat, complete with curtains as 'sails'.

'Yes, it's a boat.' Watching the delight on his face lifted

her spirits and she had to concede that the room was beautiful. A little boy's dream.

A window seat was padded with overstuffed, beautifully appliquéd cushions, each reflecting the nautical theme. Baskets overflowed with toys and shelves were stacked with more books than the average bookstore.

'Your daddy doesn't understand the word "moderation",' Fia muttered, and with that single thought her mind, which she'd managed to distract for all of five minutes, was right back in the night before. No, he certainly didn't understand moderation. But she'd been as bad, hadn't she? Wall, floor, shower—

'Mamma red—' Luca looked at her and she blinked and snapped herself back to the present.

'Mamma hot.' She took his hand and went next door to what was presumably intended as a guest bedroom. It was a pretty room, with a tiny balcony and a view overlooking the private cove beneath the villa.

'Mamma sleep here,' Luca said happily, crawling onto the bed and bouncing on it.

Fia stared at him for a long moment and then smiled. 'Yes,' she said slowly. 'Mamma sleep here. What an excellent idea.'

There was no earthly reason why they had to share a bed.

While Luca ran back to his bedroom and set about turning the place upside down, she removed her clothes from the master suite and transferred them to the spare bedroom. Then she bathed Luca, who now had his own nautical bathroom to match his nautical bedroom, read to him and then allowed Gina to take over so that she could return to the restaurant for evening service.

A hectic evening improved her mood. She hadn't seen or heard from Santo all day, presumably because he was equally busy with his project to bring the Beach Club up to the standard of the rest of the group. Maybe this could work, she thought. If she played it very, very carefully, she wouldn't even see him. And if she kept very, very busy she might even stop thinking about him every second of the day.

Testing that theory, she plunged herself into her work, creating dishes, talking to her customers, interacting with her staff. By the time she'd finished for the evening, it was late.

She walked across the sand back to the villa, pausing for a moment to look at the boathouse that had provided her with sanctuary on so many occasions when she was younger. It stood at the far end of their private beach, but Fia couldn't bring herself to go there. She couldn't bring herself to confront the memories. She'd known loneliness before but she was fast discovering that there was nothing quite as lonely as a cold, empty marriage. And hers was still in its infancy.

The villa was silent. Gina had clearly retired to bed in the staff apartment, which was situated in an annexe.

Of Santo there was no sign.

Relieved to avoid confrontation, Fia settled herself in the guest bedroom. She took a shower and slid into the large, comfortable bed, her legs aching with tiredness after a day on her feet.

She was already drifting off when the door crashed opened, flooding the room with light.

Santo stood silhouetted in the doorway, his eyes homing in on her like a hunter locating his escaped quarry. 'Just for the record,' he said smoothly, 'hide-and-seek is a game for children, not adults.'

'I wasn't playing hide and seek.'

'Then what the hell are you doing in here? When I come home from work I don't expect to have to search for you.' The combination of his lethal tone and the darkening of those eyes sent nerves fluttering through her.

'You were expecting me to wait up and bring you your slippers?' He was so extreme, she thought. Another man might have waited until morning, or just opened the door and had a civilized conversation. Not Santo. He virtually broke it down.

He prowled into the room, circling the bed like a dangerous animal gauging the best method of attack. 'Did you really think I'd let you sleep here?'

'It is my choice where I sleep,' Fia muttered, holding the silk sheets firmly around her, which was ridiculous, of course, because nothing so flimsy would protect her from a man like Santo.

'You made that choice when you married me. You'll sleep in my bed tonight and every other night.' Moving so swiftly she didn't have time to react, he ripped the sheet from her fist and scooped her into his arms.

'Get off me! Stop behaving like a caveman.' She twisted in his grip but he simply grasped her more tightly, his superior strength making it impossible for her to escape. 'You'll wake Luca!'

'Then stop yelling.'

'He'll see!'

'And what he will see is his father carrying his mother to bed,' Santo growled, as he strode towards the master suite, 'which is a perfectly acceptable scenario. I have no problems with him knowing his parents sleep together.' Kicking the door shut behind him, he walked over to the enormous bed and deposited her in the middle of it.

'For God's sake, Santo—'

'Let me give you some tips about how to make a marriage work. First, withholding sex is not going to improve my mood,' he said coldly. 'Second, I can have you flat on your back within five seconds of making the effort so let's cut the pretence. It's one of the few things we have in common.'

'You think you're so irresistible.' Fia shot upright, intending to run for the door, but he came down over her, flattening her to the bed with his superior weight, pinning her arms above her head with one hand.

She squirmed under the weight of him. 'What are you *doing*?'

'Bed sex,' he purred, his eyes glinting into hers, his mouth hovering just above hers. 'The one thing we haven't actually experienced yet. I'm a sucker for new experiences, aren't you?'

'I don't want bed sex.' She gritted her teeth and averted her face, ignoring the rush of heat in her pelvis. 'I don't want sex at all.'

'You are just making a scene because you are scared about the way I make you feel.'

'You make me feel like filleting you with my sharpest knife.'

He laughed.

Her hands were trapped by his and she tried to twist her head away from him but he caught her chin in his other hand and held her still as he slanted his mouth over hers.

The skilled brush of his lips sent shards of heat shooting through her. She moaned and writhed under him. 'I don't want to sleep in the same bed as you.'

'Don't worry about that. The sleeping part is going to come much, *much* later.' His free hand slid under her nightdress and she struggled to free her hands and defend herself from what was coming but he held her trapped.

Warmth flooded through her as she felt his hand move between her legs. 'Let me go!'

His answer to that was to slide his fingers inside her.

Heat exploded. Unable to free her hands, all she could do was try and move her hips but moving simply intensified the searing excitement caused by his intimate invasion.

'*Cristo*, I have thought about nothing but this all day,' he groaned, capturing her mouth with his and subjecting her to an explicit kiss. 'I haven't been able to concentrate. I've been talking rubbish and I couldn't make any decisions, something that has *never* happened to me before. Obviously you were the same.'

'I wasn't the same—' It was the frantic protest of a drowning person. 'I haven't thought about you once all day—'

'You're a terrible liar.'

She discovered that he could smile and kiss her at the same time and if anything that smile made the whole experience all the more erotic because it changed the way his lips moved on hers.

'I'm not a liar.' Squirming, she tried to get free of him. 'I have been too busy to give you a single thought. And why would I? It's not as if we've shared anything special.'

'No?' He released her hands and slid down the bed, sliding her thighs apart, exposing her to his darkened gaze.

Fia moaned and tried to close her legs but his hands held her firmly and her moan turned to a sob of pleasure as his tongue explored that part of her with lethal accuracy.

Her body on fire, she tried to move her hips to relieve the ache but he held her captive while his tongue subjected her to erotic torture.

Pleasure came in a dark, rushing force and she felt it build inside her to dangerous levels.

'You're so hot I can't even think when I'm with you—' His voice raw, Santo eased himself over her shifting, thoroughly excited body and thrust himself deep.

And then he stilled. He stayed like that, buried deep inside her, jaw clenched at the control needed not to move.

Fia gave a sob. 'What are you doing? Please—' Her hands scraped down his back as she urged him to move but he stayed still, his control stretched to the limit as he waited for her to come back from the edge.

'I don't want you to come yet,' he said tightly, his mouth brushing over hers in an explicit kiss. 'I want you desperate.'

She could feel the hard throb of him inside her, his erection silken smooth and powerful as the rest of him. Her breathing grew shallow. She gave a faint whimper. But still he didn't move. And she knew he was struggling too. The muscles of his shoulders were pumped up and hard, his own breathing ragged as he held on to control.

'Santo—' she raked her nails down that luscious golden skin, over those powerful muscles '—please.' Her body was burning up, nothing mattered, nothing, except this. 'Please—'

His response to her plea was to slide his hand beneath her bottom and bury himself deeper still. 'Did you think of me today?'

She barely managed to speak. 'Yes. All the time.'

'And did you find it hard to concentrate?' His voice was husky and thickened with desire and she gave a desperate moan.

'*Yes*. Santo, please—'

He held her there, just short of that place she wanted to go, until she would have done anything for the release she craved.

Just when she thought she couldn't take it any longer, he moved, slowly at first, controlling the rhythm with ruthless precision, knowing exactly how to give her maximum pleasure.

At his urging, Fia wrapped her legs around his hips, arched against him and lost herself in the madness of it. And he lost himself too. Somewhere in the swirling pleasure she was aware that control had left him and instinct had taken over.

Her climax exploded, ripping through her whole body like a storm and she heard him utter a throaty groan before the spasms of her body drew him over the same edge.

Fia had never known pleasure like it. The pulsing heat of

him accelerated her own excitement and she sobbed his name as she clung to him and rode out that storm.

Afterwards, he rolled onto his back, taking her with him. His eyes were closed. 'I like bed sex.'

Fia felt dazed and stupid. 'You made me beg.'

'I *made* you? How?' His eyes stayed closed. 'Did I threaten you?'

She covered her eyes with her hand. 'You know what I mean.'

'You mean I gave you unimaginable pleasure.' He tugged her hand away from her face, a wicked smile curving his sensuous mouth. 'You're welcome, *tesoro*.'

He was so sure of himself, so arrogantly confident in everything he did that it made her feel a thousand times worse. 'I don't want you to do that again,' she blurted out, her face hot. 'Sex is one thing, but when you do *that*—'

'Do what?'

His eyes laughed into hers and she would have looked away but he caught her chin in his fingers so all she could do was glare at him.

'You know what.'

'Oral sex?'

She burned from head to foot. 'I don't want you to do it.'

'Why? Because it makes you feel vulnerable? Good.' His voice was a soft purr. 'When you're in my bed, I want you vulnerable. And it's OK to tell me what you like, although if you're really uncomfortable with that, that's fine too because I don't need your help to know when I'm turning you on.'

'Because you're such an expert, of course.'

'You drew blood with your nails, *angelo mia*,' he said drily. 'That was a bit of a clue. And what is wrong with being an expert? You would prefer a man who fumbles?'

'I cannot believe we're having this conversation,' she mumbled and he laughed, and rolled her under him again.

'You are full of contradictions. Bold one moment and shy the next. Two women in one body.' His tone suggestive, he slid his hand lower. 'What more can a man ask for?'

Worn out by Santo's demands and the violence of her own response, she slept late and then woke and panicked about Luca.

She sprang out of bed and sprinted along to his bedroom, only to be told by a besotted Gina that Santo had got his son dressed and given him breakfast before leaving for work.

'He's the perfect man,' Gina said dreamily, 'and you are so lucky.'

Fia ground her teeth. She didn't feel lucky. She felt stupid and brainless. He only had to touch her and she turned into a quivering fool. True, he'd pinned her down so at the beginning she hadn't had much choice, but by the end he wasn't pinning her and had she slapped him? Had she told him to take his arrogant self and sleep somewhere else? No. She'd begged.

Returning to the bedroom, Fia sank back onto the tangled sheets and covered her face with her hands, utterly humiliated by the memory.

She'd begged. She'd fed his already overfed ego. She'd made him feel like a sex god.

Her phone rang. She picked it up. 'Yes?'

His dark drawl came down the phone. 'How are you feeling?'

Stupid? 'Fine, thanks.'

'You were wiped. I let you sleep in.'

Because he'd turned her into a mindless wreck. 'Thanks.' But she couldn't bring herself to hang up. Holding the phone tightly, she held her breath, hoping that he'd suggest taking her to lunch or something. A picnic on the beach? Anything that might indicate he was interested in developing a side of their relationship that wasn't about sex.

'Get some rest today. I will see you tonight.' That statement was clearly supposed to fill her with warmth and anticipation. Instead it filled her with despair.

He didn't have any feelings for her and yet she couldn't wait for him to come home.

Utterly miserable, she poured all her love and affection into her son. At least that relationship was good and it was some consolation to observe Luca's delight at the presence of his father. It was impossible to feel this had been a bad decision when she saw the two of them together.

And so a new routine started. A naturally early riser, Santo took to sharing breakfast with Luca, allowing Fia an extra hour in bed. And she needed it because whatever problems they might have, they had none in the bedroom. And she schooled herself to switch off that part of herself that craved emotional warmth. And if keeping the barrier up between them made it hard to interact with him on any other level, then that was made easier by the fact she hardly saw him during the day. He'd taken personal charge of the redevelopment of the hotel and spent each and every day there, overseeing everything. She cooked Luca an early lunch and ate with him before she started the madness of lunchtime service. Then she handed him over to Gina while she concentrated on the busiest time of her day. Her own business was flourishing. The chef who had helped out when her grandfather had been in hospital continued to help and she found it stimulating to work with someone who'd had formal training.

It was a Monday afternoon, two weeks after they'd moved into their new home, when Fia finally felt able to take a full afternoon off. Having finished lunchtime service and experimented with two new dishes, she left her team to finish the preparation for the evening and took Luca back to the villa. Confident that Santo would be fully occupied at work as he always was, she changed into a bikini and took Luca into the beautiful pool that she only ever used when Santo was safely out of the way.

Luca clung to her as she slid into the water. Kicking his legs in the water, he looked beyond her. 'Papà.'

'Papà's working,' Fia said happily, holding him firmly round the waist.

'Not any more he isn't.' Santo's cool drawl came from the edge of the pool and she spun round, horrified to find him standing there with his phone in his hand. From his polished handmade shoes to his beautifully cut suit, everything about him shrieked of spectacular success. But it wasn't the intimidating businessman that made her shiver, it was the raw sex appeal that lurked under the veneer of smooth sophistication. He dropped his phone onto the nearest sun lounger. 'That looks like a good thing to do on a hot afternoon. I'll join you.'

'Join us?' Self-conscious in her bikini, Fia held Luca in front of her. 'You're in a suit.'

A sardonic smile touched his mouth as he shrugged off his jacket and removed his tie with a few flicks of his fingers. 'Not for much longer.'

She had no intention of arguing with him. She didn't want him to stay around long enough to argue. What was he doing here? She never saw him in the middle of the day. Never. 'D-don't you need to go back to work?'

'I'm the boss.' The shirt followed the jacket. 'I decide when I work. And I always spend a few hours with Luca every afternoon before his nap. This is our time together.'

This was news to Fia. '*Every* afternoon?'

'Of course. Why are you surprised? I have no intention of being an absent father.'

She had no idea that he'd been spending every afternoon with their son. 'How do you find time for that? You have a punishing workload.'

'And a competent workforce who can manage while I play with my son for an hour.'

'You didn't tell me.'

'I have missed out on almost two and a half years of my son's life,' he said quietly. 'Is it wrong to want to catch up and spend quality time with my family?'

'No.' Guilt stabbed her. 'It's nice for Luca. Obviously I'll leave you together.' Trying not to mind that her afternoon with her son had been hijacked, she started to move towards the steps but Santo frowned.

'Where are you going?'

'You said you wanted to spend quality time with your family.'

'Which includes you.' His eyes lingered on her pink cheeks. 'Why would you think otherwise? You are too sensitive. I was stating a fact, *not* trying to make you feel guilty.'

'It will be nice for Luca to spend time with you.' It annoyed her that she felt so weak whenever he was near. Her legs trembled and her stomach fluttered with an excitement that never quite went away when he was around. 'But honestly the two of you should focus on each other and I'll just—'

'—you'll just stay right there or I'll throw you back into the pool myself.' Naked now apart from a pair of boxer shorts, he strolled over to the pool house and emerged moments later wearing a pair of swim shorts.

Fia's mouth dried.

His dark gaze clashed with hers for a moment and he gave a faint smile.

'We can do this,' he drawled, averting his eyes from her body as he walked to the edge of the pool. 'We can occupy the same space and not strip each other naked.'

'Nekkid—' Luca said happily, mimicking his father, and Fia winced.

'You have to be careful what you say. He copies everything.

Usually the words you don't want him to copy.' Holding Luca close, she backed into the shallow end, waiting for Santo to execute a flashy dive. She'd once spent an entire day watching while he and his brother had dived off the rocks further up the bay. She knew he had all the skills necessary to impress her so it came as a surprise when instead he slid into the water. And her surprise must have shown because he lifted an eyebrow in her direction. 'Given that children invariably detect tension in an adult, it might be advisable not to look at me as if a shark has just arrived in the pool.'

'I thought you were going to dive. I didn't want you to splash him.'

'This is water, *tesoro*. The idea is to get wet.'

'I don't want him to be scared and put off for ever.'

'Is that what happened to you? I've noticed that you never go in the sea.'

'My brother used to pull me under and hold me there.'

Something flickered in his eyes. Sympathy? Anger?

She waited for him to say something derogatory about her family but instead he ducked under the water and emerged right in front of her. 'Swimming is all about confidence. We need to build up your confidence. And in the meantime I will teach him that the water is fun. My brother and I spent hours swimming when we were young.' Clearing the water from his eyes, he peeled Luca away from her and switched to Italian, talking constantly to his son as he bounced him in the water, making a point of splashing him and getting the child's face wet. And Luca loved every second, including the moment his father dunked him under the water. He came up gasping and then splashed his father back, enjoying himself so much that Fia felt an agonizing pang of guilt.

She'd almost deprived him of this. She'd made a horrible, terrible misjudgement. 'I'm sorry,' she blurted out and Santo stilled, his hands firm on his son.

'Sorry for what?'

'I…I was wrong not to tell you. I thought I was doing the right thing. I thought I was protecting him because I didn't want him to have the sort of childhood I had. But now I can see—' she broke off '—you're really good with him. 'He loves being with you.'

'And that should be a cause for celebration, no? So why are you looking so gloomy?'

'Because you're never going to forgive me,' she said wearily. 'It's always going to be between us.'

He stared at her for a long moment and his mouth tightened. 'You are talking like a Baracchi, not a Ferrara. It is the Baracchi way to bear grudges and stew in a simmering broth of past discontentment. But you are now a Ferrara so you will solve this the Ferrara way and that means moving on. The past is only of relevance if we learn from it. If not, then it has no relevance in our future.'

But what *was* their future?

Could they really sustain a family based on what they had? She loved Luca. He loved Luca. They were only spending time together now because she'd inadvertently encroached on the time he spent with his son.

But even knowing that didn't change the fact that right now they felt like a family and the emotion hit her in the chest with brutal force. This was what she'd wanted as a child, and she wanted it no less now that she was an adult.

Transferring Luca to his shoulders, Santo watched her steadily. 'It's only fair to warn you that if you leave this pool now I'll just haul you back.'

'How did you know I was going to do that?'

'Because I can read the signals. You always have one eye on an escape route.'

'We both know this is your time with Luca.' She turned scarlet, wishing she'd never started this conversation. 'You never spend time with me during the day. You get up early to be with Luca, you spend time at work and then more time with him, and then you come to bed and have—' she glanced at Luca and moderated her language '—we sleep together. That's our relationship. I'm someone you spend time with in the dark.'

There was a long, tense silence.

Santo drew in a long breath. 'Firstly, I get up early and spend time with Luca because he is an early riser and I am trying to give you more rest because you work extremely hard and I respect that. Secondly, I spend time at work because I am in the middle of an important project, *not* because I am avoiding you and as you are also working hard I didn't see that as a problem. Thirdly, I come to bed and have sex with you because that is the only time of day our paths seem to cross. I don't see you as someone to have sex with in the dark, but as my wife. And if daylight sex is what it's going to take to prove to you that I'm serious about this relationship, then I have no problem with that.'

'Sex,' Luca said happily, tugging his father's hair, and Santo gave a murmur of contrition and threw her a look of exasperated apology.

'*Mi dispiace*—I'm sorry—'

'My fault. I started the conversation. He's like a sponge. Just don't say it again. With any luck he'll forget.'

What might have happened next she didn't know because Luca reached out his arms to her and almost toppled into the pool. Santo caught him deftly and scooped the child off his shoulders. 'Your mamma is planning to run and you are in charge of stopping her,' he drawled, handing the child to Fia. But, instead of releasing his father, Luca kept one arm around his shoulders and reached out the other to Fia.

Accepting the hug meant moving closer to Santo. His bare

leg brushed against hers. His eyes flicked to hers. Wry amusement danced there.

Her stomach flipped. 'He needs toys,' she blurted out. 'Toys for the pool.'

'Of course he does.' His eyes were still on hers, mocking her because he knew she was trying to change the subject. 'We will go shopping this afternoon.'

'He still has a sleep in the afternoon.'

As if to prove that statement, Luca, exhausted after such an energetic afternoon, flopped his head onto his father's bare bronzed shoulder and closed his eyes.

'I'll put him in his bed.' Somehow Santo managed to ease himself from the pool without waking the sleeping child.

Fia watched him cross the terrace and then left the pool herself and took a quick shower in the pool house.

She was just wrapped in a towel when Santo appeared behind her.

'He didn't even stir. I envy his ability to fall asleep so easily.'

He looked so impossibly gorgeous that Fia simply stared. 'Right. Well, I'll just go and—'

'You're not going anywhere.' His mouth came down on hers and he gave the towel a sharp tug.

She made an abortive grab for it as it slid to the floor. 'What are you doing?'

'Proving to you that our relationship isn't just about nighttime sex.' His voice was a sensual purr and his hands slid down the length of her spine and pressed her against him. 'You're about to experience daytime sex.'

'Santo—'

'Wall sex, floor sex—' he kissed her neck '—shower sex, bed sex—' his mouth trailed lower '—how do you feel about pool sex?'

'Absolutely not—' she moaned as his fingers found that

most sensitive part of her. 'I wouldn't be able to look the staff in the eye ever again.'

'So I'll fire them and then you won't have to.' A wicked glint in his eyes, he captured her mouth with his. 'Turn around.'

'What?'

'I have a better idea than pool sex. Sun lounger sex. Bend over.' He turned her and Fia gave a soft gasp as he bent her forward. Tipped off balance, she put her hands flat on the sun lounger, a movement that exposed her bare bottom. Feeling horribly vulnerable, she tried to stand but he pressed down on her spine and kept her there.

'I'm not going to hurt you,' he said softly. 'Just relax and trust me.'

'Santo…we can't…' she moaned, but his fingers were already stroking her there, teasing and exploring while showing a total disregard for her modesty. And within seconds she forgot about modesty. Just when she thought she'd go crazy, she felt the heat of his shaft against her and his strong hands grasped her hips and held her still as he slid deep. His throaty groan mingled with her soft gasp.

'*Cristo*, you feel incredible—'

Fia couldn't respond. Her shaking thighs were locked against the hardness of his, and he was all heat and power, each driving thrust sending her closer and closer to her own climax. It came in a rush of heat that engulfed them both simultaneously and she would have collapsed if he hadn't been holding her. With a rough laugh, he eased out of her, scooped up her quivering body and carried her into the shower. 'Great idea of yours,' he said huskily, lowering her to her feet and turning on the jet of water. 'Daytime sex. Yet another reason to leave my desk. At this rate I will not win my bet.'

'Bet?' Still dazed, she pushed her hair out of her face as the water cascaded over both of them. 'What bet?'

'That I can make the Ferrara Beach Club the most success-ful hotel in our group.' He squeezed shampoo into his palm and gently massaged her hair. 'I would never admit this to him, but my brother is a very hard act to follow. When he took a back seat in the company a year ago everyone assumed I would just hold the reins and not change anything, but care-taking someone else's baby doesn't interest me. I have more respect and admiration for my brother than any man alive, but I want to prove that I, too, have something to add to this company.'

Lulled by the gentle stroke of his fingers, Fia closed her eyes. 'You're so competitive.'

'*Sí*, it is partly that, but not entirely.' His voice soft, he turned off the shower and reached for a towel. 'When our father died it was Cristiano who took over. I was in my last year of school. He was studying in the States. He gave up everything, came home and took over as head of the family. My father's business was always small, but Cristiano took it and turned it into a global player. Because of him, Dani and I stayed in school and finished our education. He sacrificed a great deal for us. I want to do well, not because I am com-petitive, although of course I am, but because I love him and want to make him proud.'

He said it so easily, Fia thought numbly, standing still as he towelled the ends of her hair dry. No embarrassment. No awkwardness or fear that such an admission might somehow diminish his masculinity. Just a simple declaration of abso-lute family loyalty and commitment, as if that was normal. And for him it was, of course. She'd seen that commitment in all the Ferraras, but from a distance, not close up. They supported each other. Their lives were woven together like a piece of cloth, stronger as a whole than it would have been as individual strands.

Only now was she understanding what a fundamentally

bad decision she'd made when she'd kept the news of her pregnancy from him. He was right, she thought miserably, that she'd thought like a Baracchi. She'd assumed that the rift between them was a scar that would never heal because that was the way her family had always dealt with things. No slight was forgiven.

It shamed her to remember how many times the Ferraras had made overtures towards her family. Always, her grandfather had taken it as an affront.

'I didn't know that about you.' She tipped her head back and rinsed her hair. 'I mean, I knew you were close to your brother, of course. But I didn't know that he'd made those sacrifices. I knew he'd built the company into something amazing but I thought that was because he just had a driven alpha personality.'

'That too.' There was humour in his eyes as he turned off the jet of water and draped a towel around her shoulders. 'But we are fortunate in that. It was Cristiano who grew the business and supported us all at a time when my family was devastated by the loss of my father. He held it all together. And now I am happy to be able to take over that role so that he can spend more time with his family.'

She remembered Cristiano at the wedding. Tall, dark and intimidating. 'He doesn't like me. He doesn't approve of the fact you married me.'

Santo hesitated. 'He doesn't approve of the fact you didn't tell me you were pregnant, but that is in the past now. He is protective of me, just as I am protective of him. I gave Laurel a hard time when they separated, mostly because I didn't understand what was going on. Truthfully a man never knows what is going on in another's marriage.'

She felt a twinge of envy. 'You're so close to your brother and sister.'

'Of course. We are a family.' He said it as a simple statement of fact. As if it couldn't possibly be in doubt.

'I like it when we talk,' she said impulsively. 'We've never really talked about normal things. Even that night—' She broke off and he frowned.

'What?'

'We didn't talk. We just…did crazy stuff and then the call came and—'

'—and your brother was dead.'

They'd never really talked about that either, had they?

'He stole your car. You could have told everyone that, but you didn't. I've never thanked you properly for not going public with that.'

'How would that have helped? I had no desire to make a bad situation worse.'

'It might have made you look better. Nonno told people you'd lent it to him. And to be honest I don't know why anyone believed that, given the history between our families—' She shrugged. 'He made you look like the reckless one and I feel really bad about that.'

'Don't. He did not want to admit that his grandson stole the car,' Santo said quietly. 'He was grief-stricken. He didn't want to see bad, only good, and I understood that.'

'People believed—'

'The people who mattered to me knew the truth. The opinion of the world in general is of no interest to me.'

And he'd been surrounded by supporters, protected by that web of family that was fundamental to who he was. Whereas she… 'It was the worst time of my life. Worse even than the day my mother left and the day my father died. I thought Nonno was going to die,' she confessed, drawing away from him and tightening the towel around her. 'For weeks he just cried. Then he blamed himself and the guilt was almost worse than the grief. And then when he couldn't bear the guilt any longer he blamed the Ferraras. He cursed your name with every breath he took. And that carried on for months after Roberto died. And then I discovered I was pregnant.'

Santo knotted a towel around his hips, dark brows locked together, eyes fixed on her face. 'It must have been very frightening. You must have felt so alone.'

'I *was* alone. I had no one to talk it through with. I didn't know what to do. Somehow, you'd become the focus of his blame. He blamed you for lending Roberto a car he couldn't handle. I told him Roberto took the keys, but he just didn't want to listen. He didn't want to believe it. Then he blamed you for driving a flashy car that was nothing but temptation for a young man like Roberto. It was frighteningly illogical. He was the only person I had left in the world and I was watching him fall apart in front of me. First his son, my father, and then his grandson.'

'It must have been an unbearable loss,' Santo breathed. 'I remember when we lost my father, it felt as if someone had ripped a hole in our family. But we had each other and you had no one.'

'After that night, I waited for you to contact me,' she confessed. 'I used to lie awake, dreaming that you'd come—'

He swore softly in Italian and gathered her against him. 'And I assumed that I was the last person you would want to see. We talked about it, Cristiano and I, and we decided that it would be more respectful to keep a distance.'

'But did you tell Cristiano about us?'

He was silent, his chin resting on her head. 'No,' he said quietly. 'I didn't tell him that part.'

'And yet you are close and tell him everything.'

'That night was—' He broke off and she nodded.

'Yes, it was. And that is why I couldn't tell you I was pregnant. If you and I had ever spoken—if we'd had any sort of friendship or relationship—maybe I would have contacted you, but I honestly wouldn't have known what to say. "Hey, do you remember that night when we had sex?"' She bit her lip and drew away slightly so that she could look at him. 'First I was so swamped in my grandfather's grief and my own I didn't even know I was pregnant, and once I found out… I honestly didn't know what to do. My grandfather wouldn't have your name spoken in the house. How was I to tell him you were the father of my child? I didn't have anyone to talk to.'

Releasing her, Santo dragged his hand over the back of his neck. 'Now I am the one feeling guilty,' he admitted in a raw tone. 'When I walked into your kitchen that day and saw Luca, I just exploded. I thought "mine", and that was all I thought. I gave no thought to your reasoning.'

'I don't blame you for that. I'm just saying that it isn't as simple as just not telling you. It was much, much more complicated than that.'

He reached out a hand and drew her towards him. 'I rushed you into this marriage—'

'"Propelled" would be a better word.' Fia leaned her forehead against his bare chest. 'It was less shotgun than supersonic. But I could have said no.'

'I wasn't prepared to hear no.' His hands stroked her shoulders and closed over her arms. 'I pushed you into it.'

'I still could have said no. I have a brain and a mouth. I didn't agree to marry you because you bullied me.'

'Then why did you?' His voice was rough. 'You were saying no and then all of a sudden you said yes. What changed your mind that day?'

Her heart was pounding. 'One of the things you said to me was that I didn't have a clue what a family should be like.'

'I had no right to say that.'

Fia gave a sad smile. 'You had every right to say that. You cared about your son. You saw my family and didn't want that for him. But what you didn't know was that I'd been studying your family and envying your family all my life. When Luca was born I did my best to create what *you* had, not what *I* had. I wanted him to have that same network of people who loved him. I found Ben and Gina who are both warm, expressive, good people. I banned my grandfather from saying bad things. I tried to give Luca that web of support that you Ferraras take for granted.'

'I see that now. And I also see that one of the reasons Luca is so friendly and trusting is because he has been surrounded by love since he was born. And to do that in such difficult circumstances…I do think that what you achieved was nothing short of amazing.' He cupped her face in his hands and kissed her gently. 'That still doesn't explain why you suddenly agreed to marry me.'

'You kissed him,' Fia said simply. 'That first morning in your apartment when you were giving him breakfast. I walked in, sure that marriage would be the wrong thing…and you were kissing Luca. And I realised that nothing I'd created could match that. I realised that what I'd been working to reproduce was right in front of me. You were his real family. And he has a right to that, and to his cousins, aunts and uncles.'

'And do you regret that decision?'

'No. Luca loves being with you. It's only been a few weeks but his life has changed so much for the better.'

'You are an incredible mother and Luca is lucky. And you? What about your life?' His tone was unsteady. 'How is this marriage working for you? How do you feel?'

How did she feel?

She felt slightly light-headed as she always did when she was with him. She felt warm inside at his unexpected compliment. She felt—

She felt glad that she was married to him. And not just because of Luca.

Seriously unsettled, she pulled away. 'I feel fine.'

'Fine? What does "fine" mean? That word tells me nothing of how you really feel.'

She loved him. Somehow, over the past few weeks, she'd fallen in love.

The sudden realisation was like a sharp blade twisting in her heart and for a moment she couldn't breathe. Oh, how stupid. *What a crazy, dangerous, reckless thing to do.*

His mouth tightened. 'The fact that you don't know how to answer tells me a lot. You are a very unselfish person. You married me because you thought it was the right thing for our son. And you should know that I am determined to make this marriage work. I truly want you to be happy. From now on we will do more together. Not just with Luca, but as a couple. I will make space in my day and so will you.'

He had misinterpreted her silence and she was grateful for that because the last thing she wanted was for him to know how she felt.

The downside was that now he felt he had to work extra hard to please her.

She was going on his 'to-do' list.

Spending time with her wasn't a pleasure, but a responsibility.

Her pride shattered, Fia pulled away. 'You're very busy—' she pulled her damp hair over one shoulder '—and I'm very busy. Let's just carry on as we were. Honestly, that suits me.'

'Well, that doesn't suit me. If this marriage is to work it has to be about us as well as Luca.'

He wanted the marriage to work for Luca's sake. He was spending time with her for Luca's sake.

Humiliation piled on humiliation.

Switching off her own emotions, Fia tried to work out how she'd react if she weren't in love with him.

What would she say if she'd entered this marriage purely for the good of her son?

Spending time with Santo wouldn't bother her, would it? In fact it would probably seem like a good idea to get to know each other better. It made sense.

'Sure,' she croaked. 'If you want to spend time together, that sounds great.'

CHAPTER EIGHT

THE following morning she was woken by a shaft of bright sunlight as Santo opened the blinds.

'Buongiorno.' Sickeningly alert and energetic, he ripped the covers from her and handed her a robe.

Still half asleep, Fia gave a whimper of protest and stuck her head under the pillow. 'What time is it?'

'Time to get up,' he said smugly. 'You mentioned that you never see me in daylight so we are rectifying that, *dormigliona.'*

'Are you calling me a sleepy-head? Because, if so, you are to blame. You shouldn't—'

'I shouldn't what? Make love to my wife for half the night?' He removed the pillow and scooped her into a sitting position. 'I can't believe how bad you are in the morning. How did you manage when you were the one who got up for Luca in the morning?'

'I was cranky, irritable and generally horrid,' she mumbled and he gave a wicked smile as he smoothed her tangled hair back from her face.

'Fortunately you weren't any of those things last night.'

Fia turned scarlet. 'Why are you here?'

'Normally I will do the early shift, and that is another benefit to our marriage. We can share the load. But today we are going to have a family breakfast.'

He was listing benefits, she thought numbly, as if he had to constantly remind himself of all the reasons this marriage was a good idea. She'd never thought of herself as romantic, but she was starting to realise she was nowhere near as practical as she would have liked to be. She would have given a lot for him to have just said he was glad he married her because he liked being with her.

He glanced at his watch. 'Breakfast first, and then I have one short meeting I can't get out of. After that we are going shopping.' Showered, shaved and dressed in a suit, he looked so indecently sexy that Fia immediately wanted to grab him and haul him back into the bed.

'I have lunchtime service.'

'Not today. I've rearranged your schedule. *Don't* be angry with me.' Anticipating her response, he dived in first. 'Normally I wouldn't dream of interfering with your business, but today is about us. I really want to spend time with you.'

No, he didn't want to. He thought he ought to. Not because he found her company addictive, but because he wanted to invest time in his marriage for Luca's sake.

That was item number four on his agenda. Spend quality daylight time with Fia.

Resigned to going along with that strategy, Fia forced herself out of bed. 'I need to take a shower.'

'No!' He moved away from her so fast he almost stumbled.

Fia stared at him in confusion. 'I can't take a shower?'

'Yes, *you* can take a shower,' he hissed through gritted teeth, 'but I'm not going to take one with you.' He retreated to the doorway. 'I promised myself that today is going to be spent out of the bedroom.'

'Right.'

'Meet us downstairs when you're dressed.' He fumbled

behind him for the door handle. 'I'll make you coffee. You take it white. I know that about you.'

'Thank you.' She probably should have been touched that he was trying so hard but instead it just depressed her to think he had to make such an effort. A relationship should be a natural thing, shouldn't it?

By the time she joined them on the terrace, Santo had removed his jacket and was engaged in conversation with his son. Warmth spread through her as it always did when she saw the two of them together.

'Mamma!' Luca's face brightened and Santo rose to his feet and pulled out her chair.

'Mamma is joining us for breakfast so we must both be on our best behaviour.'

Fia kissed Luca and lifted her eyebrows as she saw the traditional Sicilian breakfast of *brioche* and *granita*. 'You made this?'

'Not exactly.' A rueful smile crossed Santo's handsome face as he sat back down. 'I ordered breakfast from the Beach Club. I want your opinion. We're losing business to you. You're going to tell me why. Is it the food? Is it the surroundings? I want to know what we're doing wrong.'

Fia sat down. 'I don't know anything about running a hotel so I'll be no help to you at all.'

'But you know a great deal about food.' He passed her a plate. 'And given that my customers would rather eat yours than mine, I assume you're in a position to have an opinion on that. I brought the menus down for you to look at.'

Fia took the menus from him and scanned them, wondering how honest she was supposed to be. 'Your menu is too broad.'

'*Scusi?*' Santo's eyes narrowed. 'You are suggesting we don't offer a choice? But choice is good. It means we can cater to a wide range of tastes.'

'You asked for my opinion. If you don't want it, don't ask.'

He breathed deeply. '*Mi dispiace.* Carry on. You were saying—?'

'It's good to have a choice, but you don't want to offer so many things that people don't know what cuisine you're serving. This is Sicily. Serve Sicilian food and be proud of it. In the Beach Shack we rely totally on local seasonal produce. If it's not in season, we don't cook it. We buy our fish fresh from the boat in the morning so we don't even choose the evening menu until we've seen what is fresh.' She reached across and took an orange from the bowl on the table. The skin was dappled dark red and purple and she picked up her knife and peeled it deftly, exposing the scarlet flesh. 'It is the temperature variation that makes these blood oranges the best in the world. That and the soil, which is perfect for growth. Our customers can see them growing next to the restaurant. We pick them fresh and juice them and I guarantee that when our guests return home they will want to buy blood oranges, but they won't be able to find anything that tastes like this.'

'So you're saying fresh and local. I understand that. But we are catering for larger numbers than you, so that degree of flexibility isn't always possible.'

'It should be. And what I don't grow, I outsource from local producers. I'll talk to my suppliers. See if they can cope with a larger order.'

Santo poured coffee. 'I want you to look over the menu properly and make suggestions.'

'Isn't that going to hurt the feelings of your head chef?' Fia handed Luca a segment to suck.

'My concern is not the feelings of my head chef but the success of the business which, ultimately, is in everyone's best interests. At the moment most of our guests prefer to eat with you.' He handed her coffee. 'Congratulations. You've just been appointed as Executive Head Chef, overseeing both the Beach Shack and the Beach Club.'

Fia gave a disbelieving laugh. 'You're a very surprising person, do you know that? All macho one minute and surprisingly forward-thinking the next. When you first mentioned marriage I assumed you were going to insist I gave up work and stayed at home.'

'Do you want to stay at home?'

Fia picked up a napkin and wiped the sticky juice from Luca's fingers. 'I love being with him, but I enjoy my work, too. I like the flexibility of the life I have and I'm proud of the fact I can support my son without financial help from anyone. But I wouldn't want to work if it meant I couldn't see him. This is a perfect compromise and I admit it's nice to have your chef helping out. I like him.'

'Now you are working with me, which means you can take off as little or as much time as you like. But not until you've told me how to improve the restaurants. Try the food.'

Fia tore a piece of the warm, buttery *brioche*, automatically studying the texture. 'I thought you'd be very traditional about a woman's role.'

'I think we have already established that we don't know enough about each other,' he said softly, 'but that is slowly changing. Now tell me what you think of the *brioche*.'

'It's good. A little greasy, perhaps.' She nibbled the corner, testing the flavour, and felt a glow of satisfaction because she knew hers was infinitely superior. And it should be. She'd worked herself to the ground perfecting the recipe. She kneaded and baked and tested until she was satisfied that it couldn't get any better. 'As we're married and I have a vested interest in your success, I'll share my secret recipe with your chef.'

Aware that he was watching her, she picked up her spoon and tasted the *granita* from the tall glass. 'Elegant presentation.' She made a mental note to review the way she served hers in the restaurant. 'It's difficult to make the perfect *granita*.'

'It's just water, sugar and, in this case, coffee.'

'The Arabs first introduced it when they flavoured snow from Mount Etna with sugar syrup and jasmine water.' She took another spoonful. 'But if it isn't frozen to the right consistency then it tastes all wrong.'

'And does this taste wrong?'

'It's not bad—' This time she scooped *granita* up with the *brioche* and tasted both together. 'I've had worse.'

He winced. 'That is not the accolade I was hoping for. So when and where did you learn to cook?'

She put the spoon down slowly. 'I taught myself. When my mother left, I was surrounded by men who expected me to cook for them. Fortunately I loved it. I made lots of mistakes and plenty of food ended up in the bin, but after a while I started to get a lot of things right and when they turned out right I wrote them down. Why are you looking at me like that?'

'You had *no* formal training?'

'Of course not. When would I have had formal training?' She poured milk into Luca's cup. 'I would have loved to go to college, to travel and spend some time with other chefs, but that was never an option.'

He gave an incredulous laugh. 'The chef who made that *brioche* trained at two of the best restaurants in Italy.'

'He probably hasn't made as many bad batches of brioche as I have. It's about experimenting. And it isn't all about training. Sometimes it's about the quality of the raw ingredients and giving the customer what they want.'

'And what do you think my customers want?'

'I only know about my own.'

'Given that a high percentage of your customers come

from my hotel, they're one and the same thing,' he drawled. 'I'm surprised your grandfather let you run the restaurant. Cooking for him is one thing, but running a business is another. He is very traditional.'

She wished he'd remove his sunglasses. With those dark shades obscuring his eyes she couldn't tell what he was thinking. 'My grandmother always had a few tables on the water's edge. Nothing fancy, but the food was always fresh and local. I suppose because she cooked for others, he was more accepting of me doing the same thing. But he does complain. He thinks I've turned it into something fancy.'

'You have had a very difficult life,' he said quietly. 'Losing both your parents and then your brother…and yet you've managed to hold it all together. Not just hold it together, but you have a thriving business, a happy child and a more mellow grandfather. You didn't repeat the pattern you saw, you created your own pattern.'

'The way you live your life is a choice,' Fia said. 'I chose to copy your family, not mine.'

'And you did that without any support. I want you to know that I do have enormous respect for what you have achieved. And I owe you an enormous apology for being so hard on you when I found out about Luca.'

'You don't have to apologise,' she muttered. 'I understand. You're very, very focused on family. I've never really had that so we sort of came at the whole thing from a different place.'

His dark eyes raked her face. 'Yes. I think we did. But we're in the same place now and that is the way it's staying.' He stood up abruptly. 'I have a meeting that will last about an hour. Then I've asked Gina to take Luca so that we can have some time alone.'

Alone sounded terrifying to Fia. Alone meant concentrating really hard on not showing him how she felt. Respect, she could take, especially from a man like Santo who didn't give it readily. Pity didn't interest her.

'Why don't we take Luca with us? Make it a family day out?'

Santo paused in the process of putting on his jacket. 'I was thinking more along the lines of something more romantic.'

'Romantic?' She managed a light-hearted laugh. 'Really, you don't need to do that. I appreciate the thought but it isn't necessary.'

'It is necessary. Apart from your wedding dress, I haven't bought you a single thing since we got together. You're my wife. You deserve the best.'

Oh, God, she was an embarrassment to him.

Why hadn't that occurred to her before?

She was married to Santo Ferrara and she was dressing the same way she'd always dressed. Mortified that he'd had to broach the topic in such a way, she caved in and nodded quickly.

'Yes, of course. Let's go shopping. Whatever you think.'

'Finish your breakfast. I'll pick you up in an hour. It's important that we spend time alone together. And you—' he bent to kiss Luca's dark hair '—are having a day with Gina. Be good.'

With a final glance at Fia, he strode off the terrace towards the hotel, leaving her staring after him in despair.

'He wants to spend the day with me because he thinks he ought to. And he's going to buy me clothes so that I look right and don't embarrass him in public. Your Auntie Dani has already told me he hates shopping so the fact that he's determined to take me must mean I'm not just a bit embarrassing but extra embarrassing.' Fia handed Luca another piece of *brioche*. 'Name one good thing about our relationship apart from you. Go one. Just one.'

'Sex,' Luca chortled helpfully and Fia gave a moan of despair and dropped her head into her hands.

'You look stunning in that.' Expending every effort to please her, Santo layered on the compliments but the more he praised, the more withdrawn she became. Having never before known a female to treat an extravagant shopping expedition with so little enthusiasm, he racked his brain to work out what he was doing wrong.

Was she disappointed that they'd left Luca at home?

'You like this?' She stared listlessly at her reflection in the mirror. Truthfully Santo liked her best in nothing at all, but he assumed that to admit that would be unlikely to improve her mood so he dutifully studied the blue silk dress and nodded.

'The colour suits you. Let's add it to the pile.'

She disappeared into the changing room to take it off and then re-emerged clutching the blue dress.

Santo took it from her and handed it to the sales assistant along with his card. 'That dress will be perfect for our family party.'

'What family party?'

'It's Chiara's birthday party in a couple of weeks. Ferrara family gathering. Cristiano adores his girls—and that includes Laurel—so you can be sure a big fuss will be made.' Santo picked up the bags in one hand and led her back to the Lamborghini. 'I thought I'd mentioned it.'

'No. No, you didn't.' She stopped dead just outside the store and Santo had to clamp her against him to prevent her from being flattened by a group of overeager shoppers.

Instead of pulling away, she stayed still in the circle of his arm, her head resting against his chest.

He frowned.

There was something intensely vulnerable about the gesture and he felt a flicker of concern.

It was the first time they'd touched like this, he realised, and he felt another flash of guilt at the way he'd treated her. He'd rushed her into marriage without giving any thought to her feelings. All he'd thought about was his son's welfare. Not once had he thought about hers.

The scent of her hair wound itself around his senses. The curve of her breast brushed against his arm. Fire shot through his body but he ignored it and forced himself to deliver a chaste kiss to the top of her head.

From now on he was going to focus on her, he vowed. 'You'll enjoy the party. It's a chance for everyone to get together.' Gently, Santo eased her away from him and brushed her hair back from her face so that he could look at her. 'My family always makes an enormous fuss about birthdays. Chiara will be six. Brace yourself for balloons and an indecent quantity of cake.' Still holding her hand, he threw the bags into the back of the car. 'The party is in their home in Taormina so we'll fly there because there is no way I'm negotiating Friday night traffic.'

'We're staying with Laurel and Cristiano?'

'Is that a problem?' He opened the door for her, trying not to focus on her legs as she slid into the passenger seat. 'Your grandfather seems to have made a good recovery and we still have a nurse there at night. If you're worried about the day, I can arrange something.'

'I'm not worried. Gina will be around.'

But Santo could tell she was lying and he searched for the cause. 'Are you finding the whole Ferrara family thing overwhelming?'

'No. I think you're all very lucky. You have a wonderful family.' She spoke as if she wasn't part of that and Santo breathed deeply as she fastened her seat belt without looking at him.

'Fia—'

Horns blared, interrupting his attempt to question her further, and he scowled and paced around to his side of the car. 'Dani and her brood will be there, too. And Laurel, of course. She's looking forward to getting to know you better. But she'll really appreciate us coming. It helps Chiara. She's only been with them a year.'

'A year?'

'Chiara is adopted. And don't ask me to tell you her history because it makes me want to punch a hole through something.' Santo started the engine and pulled into the fast moving traffic, driving as only a Sicilian could. 'When she first came to live with them she wasn't really used to people. She certainly wasn't used to people being kind to her. They were very patient, but it was little Elena who broke through that wall she'd built. Try telling a two-year-old that her new big sister just wants to be left alone—it doesn't work. And now they're the best of friends, as siblings should be.' He spoke without thinking and then saw a flicker of something in her eyes and cursed himself. Here he was, talking about siblings, and her brother was dead. '*Mi dispiace. Cristo*, I'm truly sorry, Fia.' He reached across and curled his fingers over hers. 'That was unbelievably insensitive of me. Forgive me.'

'There's nothing to forgive. I didn't have that sort of relationship with my brother and there is no sense in pretending that I did. My family is nothing like yours. And I don't want you to feel you have to tread carefully around the topic.'

Without releasing her hand, Santo took a sharp right turn and pulled into a narrow street. His fingers tightened on hers. 'My family is your family, *tesoro*. You are a Ferrara now.'

She stared straight ahead. 'Yes.'

Maybe it was taking her time to accept that, he thought.

Maybe after a few family gatherings she'd realise that she was part of it.

'I could make Chiara's birthday cake.' She blurted the words out as if she wasn't sure the suggestion would be welcome. 'But if they'd rather do their own thing—'

'No. I think that would be very well received. If you're sure it isn't too much for you on top of everything else.' Maybe that was what was wrong, he mused. She was working hard in the restaurant as well as looking after Luca.

Santo let go of her hand and drove for a few minutes before pulling up outside a small restaurant that had been his favourite for years. 'Today you are going to eat food that someone else has cooked for you. This place is incredible. Even you will be impressed.'

He needed to spend more time with her, he realised. He needed to make sure that their relationship wasn't just about sex.

He chose a quiet table in the corner of the courtyard, shaded by the tangled leaves of a mature vine. The tantalizing aroma of garlic and spices drifted from the kitchen and the sounds of sizzling mingled with the hum of conversation and the occasional raised voices of the chefs.

They ordered a selection of dishes to share and Santo watched as she tasted each one. At one point she went into the kitchen to question the chef and then pulled a notebook out of her bag and scribbled in it.

She was an instinctive cook, he realised, finding it a pleasure to watch her sample flavours and textures.

'This is good. But I'd make it without the pine nuts—' she dissected the food with her fork to study the composition '—and possibly lighter on the spices because they're overwhelming the flavour of the fish. If we served it with a green salad it would be a perfect healthy lunch for the Beach Club. And I've been thinking about that—'

'About the menu at the Beach Club?'

'You want to attract a young, sports-mad crowd. So you should serve a mixture of light, healthy food and a few pasta dishes that deliver carbohydrate without thick calorie-rich sauces. Increase the fish and vegetables. The current menu looks like a homage to comfort food.' She scribbled more notes for herself and he watched, thinking how much he'd underestimated her.

'Would you be willing to review the menus for the whole Ferrara Group?'

Her cheeks turned pink. 'Would you want me to?'

'Definitely. Whenever we build a new hotel, Laurel oversees the development of each fitness centre. She advises us on equipment and she helps us find the right staff.'

She put her pen down and picked up her fork. 'Is that how Cristiano met Laurel? She worked for you?'

'She was Dani's best friend at college and I employed her as my personal trainer. Cristiano was so impressed he asked her to advise on all our fitness centres. I never thought I would see Cristiano fall crazily in love, but he did. When he and Laurel split for a while he was like a different person. It was a great relief to everyone when they got back together. They never stopped loving each other and it was their love that held them together.'

She stopped eating.

Slowly, she put her fork down on her plate as if she could no longer face the food.

All the happiness seemed to have drained out of her.

Santo rewound the conversation in an attempt to work out what he'd said. Maybe she'd misinterpreted his story. 'So basically Cristiano was not willing to entertain the idea of divorce because he loved her so much.'

'That's romantic.' Her face was horribly pale and she sat

back and gave up the pretence of eating. 'This is delicious but I'm not very hungry. I'm sorry.'

'There is no need to be so polite. But a moment ago you were chatting happily and now you look as if I delivered bad news.' She'd been fine until he mentioned Cristiano's name. Aware that Cristiano had been cool with her at the wedding, Santo made a mental note to warn his brother to lighten up. 'If something is wrong, I wish you would just tell me.'

'Nothing is wrong. I'm having a really nice day. Just a bit tired.'

If she was tired, then that was his fault, Santo thought as they left the restaurant. Guilt flashed through him. They spent a substantial chunk of every night making love. He'd thought she enjoyed the physical side of their relationship as much as he did, but now he was wondering whether she just saw that as another one of her duties. He made a mental note to let her sleep through the night instead of keeping her awake.

He was all too conscious that he was the one who had propelled her into this marriage.

She'd married him because she felt she had a responsibility towards Luca.

Was she regretting that now?

Their marriage limped along for another few weeks with Santo going out of his way to fulfil the role of perfect husband. He showered her with expensive gifts, took her on glamorous nights out, even flew her to Paris to sample the food in a restaurant she'd mentioned. But the harder he tried, the worse she felt. Santo took to coming to bed later and later and when he did eventually slide into the bed next to her, he didn't touch her.

For Fia, it was the final straw.

The one thing that had always been good about their marriage was the sex, and apparently he no longer even wanted that. She was well aware that, before he'd married her, Santo didn't have a history of long relationships. He had a short attention span when it came to women, was easily bored and had a ferocious sex drive. No matter what he'd said at the beginning, it was obvious to her that he'd had enough of sleeping with the same woman.

And as far as she could see, that could have only one outcome.

Hadn't he told her right at the beginning that sex was one of the most important things to him? Hadn't he had confidence in the success of their marriage because they'd been so compatible?

If that part was over, what did they have left?

No matter what he said, there was no way a Ferrara would endure a sexless marriage.

He would take a lover, and that would be harder to handle than anything she'd had to handle in her life before.

Lack of sex, and the implications behind that proved more of a sleep disturber than too much sex and Fia grew more and more tired.

During the day she threw herself into her work. She spent time at the Beach Club and made some suggestions for changes that she thought would increase the popularity of the restaurant. She increased the volume of seating outside and altered the menu. When Santo told her that bookings had doubled, she was happy because she wanted so badly to please him.

Only with Luca could she really relax and then only if Santo was too busy to join them.

She took to checking his schedule so that she could be sure to pick times when he was tied up in meetings.

But Chiara's birthday party was looming and there was no avoiding the big Ferrara family gathering. Fia knew that seeing Cristiano and Laurel together would simply emphasize the cracks in her own marriage. Cristiano and Laurel were bound together by love. She and Santo were bound together by Luca.

Perhaps going away as a family might be good for them, Fia thought bleakly.

The plan was that after the party in the afternoon, the adults were going out to dinner and she squashed down her nerves and told herself that this would be a chance to get to know his family. And an excuse to add some glamour to her life.

Conscious that she spent a large proportion of her day dressed in unflattering chef's whites, she decided that this would be the perfect opportunity to wear one of the dresses Santo had insisted on buying her. She tried to remember which one had attracted the most enthusiastic response from him and in the end decided to wear the blue silk.

When she tried it on it felt and looked so good that her spirits lifted. Maybe things weren't as bad as she thought.

No marriage was perfect all the time, was it?

Santo was under a lot of pressure at work and taking a few hours out every day to spend 'quality time' with her simply increased that pressure. It was no wonder he had to work late.

They flew by helicopter, much to Luca's excitement, landing in the grounds of Cristiano's luxury palazzo in the hills above the pretty town of Taormina. From here she could see Mount Etna, and beneath her the sparkling expanse of the Mediterranean.

'This is Laurel's favourite place.' Santo urged her towards the terrace, carefully carrying the box containing the cake Fia had made. 'She had a difficult childhood and was brought up in care so she'd never had a home of her own. Cristiano bought this for her as a surprise.'

He loved his wife so much he'd bought her the one thing she'd never had—a beautiful home.

What would it be like, Fia wondered, *to be loved like that*?

As they rounded the corner she felt daunted by the number of people. 'Who are they all?'

He scanned heads. 'The man by the tree is my uncle and the woman next to him is his wife. The two women supervising the pool are cousins of mine—they work in marketing for the company—' the list was endless and then he moved on to the children '—Rosa is the one in the pool, you already met her with Dani. Chiara and Elena are together under the tree and the rest are children of cousins, friends, people we know—' He shrugged dismissively and she thought again how different his life was from hers.

'Fia!' Looking as lean and fit as ever, Laurel walked up to her and kissed her on both cheeks. 'Welcome. Isn't it hot? I just want to go and lie down in the air-conditioning. Chiara is feeling a bit overwhelmed, I'm afraid. I'm starting to wish we'd kept it smaller.'

'Does smaller exist for a Ferrara?'

Laurel laughed. 'Good point. Are you finding this family overwhelming too? I know I did. Fortunately you get used to it.'

The difference was that Laurel had a husband who adored her.

'I made the cake. I hope it's all right.' Feeling ridiculously nervous, Fia removed the lid of the box and Laurel gasped as she saw the cake.

'Oh, my goodness, it's perfect! A fairy castle—' Delight spread across her face. 'How did you *do* that?'

'I used the picture you sent me of her favourite toy.'

'The fairies even have wands—' Laurel's tone was awed as she examined the detail '—and wings. How did you make the wings?' Her response was everything Fia had hoped for.

'Spun sugar. I broke quite a few trying to get them right.'

Santo pulled a face. 'I'm expected to eat a pink turret and

fairy wings?' But he smiled at Fia. 'Very clever. And now I'm going to put it down because I don't want to be the one who drops it.'

He put it in the centre of the table.

From a distance, Chiara saw the cake and her eyes grew huge with wonder.

'She's too shy to come and investigate,' Laurel said. 'It's because she doesn't know you.'

In the end it was bouncy little Elena who dragged her big sister across the terrace towards the amazing cake.

'Elena never lets her out of her sight,' Laurel told Fia. 'She has her own room, but she crawls into Chiara's bed every night. She just adores her big sister.'

And the affection was clearly returned, although Chiara was less openly demonstrative.

'This is only her second birthday with us,' Laurel murmured. 'She didn't even know what a birthday was before she came to us, so if she doesn't do or say the right thing, please forgive her.'

Fia's eyes filled. Mortified, she blinked back the tears but not before Laurel had noticed.

'I'm so sorry.' Embarrassed, Fia pulled herself together. 'I don't know what's wrong with me at the moment. Not enough sleep or something.'

'Don't apologise. I cry on a regular basis when I think how lonely her life was. It's hard not to just want to give her everything, but of course all she really needs is love and stability.'

And it was obvious that she had that.

Chiara thanked her shyly for the cake but the real thanks was the look on her face as she examined each part of her fairy castle.

Cristiano strode over to join them and scooped up both his

daughters, one on each arm. 'Which one of you is the birth-day girl?'

Holding tightly to the man who was now her father, Chiara blushed shyly. 'Me.'

'Then it's time to come and greet your guests and make them welcome in true Ferrara style, young lady. And then we can cut that fantastic cake.'

Chiara wrapped her arms tightly around his neck. 'Will you come too?'

Fia saw the emotion in Cristiano's eyes. 'Of course,' he said softly. 'I am your *papà*. Where else would I be but by your side?' He smiled at Fia with genuine warmth. 'Welcome. And thank you for that spectacular cake. It was very thought-ful of you to make her something so special.'

It was a crazy, happy afternoon and when it came to bed-time Luca chose to sleep in a room with Chiara, Elena and Rosa.

Laurel rolled her eyes in disbelief. 'I'm so sorry. Are you OK with that? We have ten bedrooms. Don't ask me why they choose to cram themselves into one.'

'I think it's fantastic.' Fia thought about how lonely she'd been as a child. What she wouldn't have given to be tucked into a cosy room with three giggling cousins.

'Truthfully? I think it's fantastic too. And you don't need to worry because Cristiano's aunt is staying the night and she has promised to watch them.' Laurel gave the children a stern look. 'Straight to sleep, no nonsense.'

Having issued that edict, they left the room and Fia caught her eye.

'They're going to be up all night.'

'I think you're right. But the upside is that they might sleep late. And now we need to get ready. This restaurant Cristiano has picked is very elegant. We're all dying to hear your opinion on the food, although I'm not sure I can eat anything after all that cake. It was the best thing I've ever tasted.'

Warmth rushed through her.

She was one of them, she thought.

She *was* a Ferrara now.

Maybe her marriage wasn't perfect, but it was still early days and Santo had been making a huge effort. Instead of wishing she could have more, she needed to make the most of what she did have. She needed to try harder. And the first thing she'd do was kick-start their sex life. In the beginning he'd found her irresistible. It was up to her to rekindle that side of their relationship.

Santo was on the terrace drinking with Cristiano and Raimondo, Dani's husband, so Fia was able to take her time getting ready.

The blue silk dress skimmed her curves and showed off her legs. Maybe she wasn't as toned as Laurel, she thought as she looked in the mirror, but she ate well and ran around all day so her figure wasn't bad.

Sliding her feet into stilettos, she picked up her purse and drew in a deep breath.

Not once so far in their relationship had she actually tried to seduce Santo. This was going to be a first.

There was a brief tap and then the door opened and Laurel and Dani stood there.

Dani tipped her head to one side and studied her. 'Oh, my poor unsuspecting brother. He doesn't stand a chance.'

With that confidence-boosting comment ringing in her ears, Fia joined them and the three women walked down to the terrace.

Santo had his back to her and nerves fluttered in her stomach as she stared at those broad shoulders.

Cristiano saw them first and immediately broke off the conversation to greet them. Although he was complimentary to all, his eyes were on his wife and Fia felt a stab of envy at the obvious depth of their love.

From the little Santo had told her, that love had held them together through dark times.

Doubt slithered its way into her happiness. What did she and Santo have? Their marriage wasn't based on anything so powerful, was it? What was going to save them if trouble came their way?

As Dani planted herself in front of Raimondo and waited for him to say the right thing, Santo turned towards Fia.

He was gorgeous, the physical attraction so powerful that Fia caught her breath. And then she noticed that those dark, sexy eyes looked tired.

He wasn't sleeping either.

'Hey—' Dani punched her brother on the arm. 'Doesn't Fia look stunning? She is Fia the fantastic. Fia the fabulous. If you don't say something nice she might just turn into Fia the ferocious so you'd better say the right thing fast. Here's a hint—something like "let's forget dinner and just go straight upstairs" would probably go down well.'

Santo rounded on her. 'You talk too much,' he snapped and Dani took a step backwards, visibly hurt by the unexpected attack.

Cristiano observed that exchange with narrowed eyes, looking first at his brother and then at Fia, who wanted to do nothing more than just go and join the cosy heap of children upstairs and hide under the covers.

So much for seducing him.

It was clear he just wasn't interested.

'We ought to go,' Laurel said quickly. 'The limo is waiting. And Fia, I want you to tell me how to cook *arancine*. Cristiano loves it and every time I try, it's a dismal failure. I swear his mother still can't work out why he married me.'

Because he loved her, Fia thought bleakly. And love filled

in all the other cracks, like rain on parched earth. She had nothing like that and the cracks in her own marriage were widening. The shaky foundations were splitting apart and soon the entire thing would collapse.

Dani slipped her arm into hers as they walked. 'I have no idea what's wrong with Santo,' she grumbled. 'I apologise for my brother. Ugh. Men! This is why a woman has to have girlfriends. Let's talk about something important. I have a party to go to next week. I'm wondering whether to try some of that magnetic nail varnish.' She chattered away and Fia was grateful for the change of subject and for the nonstop talk that didn't require her input.

The evening was a success because of the efforts of the others, but somehow those efforts made Fia all the more aware of those widening cracks.

Despite the time she'd taken to look her best, Santo barely glanced at her, instead choosing to talk business with his brother and brother-in-law while Fia felt invisible.

If she still didn't attract his interest then that was it, wasn't it?

And if that part of their relationship was over, then the rest of it was over, too.

Whatever he said about marriage being for ever, there was no way a physical guy like Santo would want to stay with a woman he was no longer attracted to.

She was going to be the first Ferrara in history to be granted a divorce.

CHAPTER NINE

'I'M sorry if you found the weekend overwhelming.' Santo was formal and polite as they arrived home the following day.

'I didn't. Your family is lovely and it was a treat for Luca to spend time with his cousins.' She kept her voice bright and breezy and was so grateful for Luca, who kept up a running commentary about his cousins.

When Santo's phone rang, she almost moaned with relief, a feeling that doubled as he told her he was going to have to go straight to his office at the hotel and do a few hours' work.

And if there was something slightly cagey about the way he was behaving, she told herself that it didn't matter anyway. Even if he was lying about the work part and was actually seeing a woman, it was irrelevant.

When she made no response, he sighed. 'I might be late. Don't wait up for me.'

Of course she wouldn't wait up for him. He'd made it clear enough that he didn't want her. 'No problem at all,' she said quickly. 'Luca and I will have a swim in the pool and an early night.'

His mouth tightened and he started to walk away when he appeared to change his mind. He turned, uncertainty flickering in his eyes.

'Fia—'

He was going to tell her that this wasn't working. He was

going to tell her that he wanted a divorce and she would make a fool of herself because she wasn't ready to hear it yet. She needed to get her head round it. She needed to make plans.

'Luca, don't do that!' Using their son as an excuse, she shot across the terrace and relieved a startled Luca of a toy that was offering no threat whatsoever.

She fussed over him for a few moments and then Luca looked past her and his face fell.

'Papà gone.'

'Yes,' Fia whispered. 'He's gone. I'm sorry. I don't know what else to do.'

'Sex,' Luca said stoutly and she pulled him into a hug.

'Tried that,' she croaked. 'Didn't work.'

Somehow she stumbled through the day. She and Luca spent some time with her grandfather and then Gina took him back to the villa while Fia worked late at the Beach Shack.

Knowing that all that was waiting for her at home was a huge, empty bed, she was in no hurry to return to the villa. Instead she did something she hadn't done for years. Not since the night when Luca was conceived.

She went to the boathouse.

The approach took her along the stretch of private beach that belonged to the Ferraras. As a child she would have been guilty of trespassing and she realised with a lurch that she was now walking on her own land.

The main doors opened straight onto the sea, and a side door allowed access from the land. Fia had always slid in through the window, but this time she paused with her hand on the door, wondering whether it was just going to make her feel worse to visit somewhere that held so many emotional memories. It wasn't an accident that she hadn't been back here. This had been her escape in bad times.

The moon sent shimmers of light across the calm sea,

providing sufficient illumination for her to see what she was doing.

It occurred to her that it would have been sensible to fetch a torch, but she reasoned that she didn't need a torch to just stare at a collapsing old pile of planks.

The boathouse had been in a state of disrepair for so long that there was always a risk of injury, but as she pulled open the door she noticed that it opened smoothly. No creaks. She slipped quietly inside. In the past her routine had been to simply sit on one of the old lobster pots that were stacked by the door and stare at the water.

Her foot slipped on something soft and she frowned down at the floor. Oil? Fabric of some sort?

She was about to bend down and investigate when the place was suddenly filled with light. Shocked to discover that the place now had electricity, she looked up to see what seemed to be hundreds of tiny fairy lights strung around the walls.

Enchanted, she was just wondering what it all meant when she heard a sound behind her.

Turning quickly, she saw Santo standing there. 'You weren't meant to arrive yet.' His thumbs were hooked into the pockets of his jeans and he looked lean, fit and more handsome than one man had a right to be. 'I hadn't quite finished.'

Finished? Confused, Fia glanced around the boathouse, seeing the changes for the first time.

The place had been transformed. Those oily, splintered planks of wood had been sanded and polished. An oil stove nestled in one corner, ready to provide heat for chilly winter evenings and in another corner was a sofa, heaped with cushions and a fur rug.

It was the cosiest, most decadent place she'd ever seen. The tiny lights twisted along the walls made the place feel like a magical grotto.

She took a step forward and again felt the softness underfoot. Glancing down, she saw rose petals. Rose petals that formed a red carpet, not towards the bed, but towards a little table. And on the table was a small, beautifully wrapped box.

Heart beating, she looked at that box and then at Santo.

'Open it.' He hadn't moved from the doorway, the expression in his eyes cautious, as if he weren't sure of his welcome.

'You've—' She looked around her, noticing a million thoughtful little touches, like the little seat that had been placed by the doors to the water. The place she'd always sat with her arms wrapped around her knees, watching the sea. Instead of an upturned box, there was a rocking chair. 'You did this?'

'I know how unhappy you are and I know that when you're unhappy you need somewhere to go and be by yourself. I'd rather you didn't feel the need to escape from me but if you do then I want you to be comfortable.'

Her eyes filled. 'Our marriage isn't working.'

'I know that, and I suppose it isn't surprising in the circumstances.' His voice was uncertain. 'I have so many things to apologise for I don't know where to start.'

It wasn't the response she'd expected. 'You could start by telling me why the place is covered in rose petals.'

He ran his hand over the back of his neck. 'Remembering the night of our wedding still shames me. As long as I live I will never be able to delete the image of you on your knees sweeping up rose petals I'd so thoughtlessly had put down. I hurt your feelings badly.'

'I just thought it was mocking our relationship. It wasn't romantic. It was never romantic.' The tears sat in her throat and didn't move. 'Those rose petals—'

'—were a manipulation on my part, I admit that. But I was manipulating the minds of those around us, not mocking you. That interpretation didn't occur to me until I walked in and found you on your knees clearing them up. You once accused me of being an insensitive bastard and I am thoroughly guilty of that charge. But it was insensitivity rooted in thoughtlessness, *not* in a conscious desire to hurt you. I put these down myself, by hand. That's why they're not even in a straight line. I've never done it before.'

'Why did you do it now?' He still didn't get it, she thought numbly. Rose petals were a romantic gesture.

'I was trying to make you happy. I wanted you to smile,' he said thickly, every plane of his body rigid with tension. 'You smile with Luca all the time and I love it when you laugh. You never do that with me. You're always jumpy and on edge and that is probably my fault.' He spread his hands in a gesture of frustration and despair. 'But I do want you to be happy. What do I have to do?'

Fia felt tears scald her eyes and this time they refused to retreat. She swallowed, but they kept coming, brimming in her eyes and then spilling over onto her cheeks.

Santo swore under his breath and strode forward, folding her in his arms so tightly that she couldn't breathe. '*Cristo*, I have never, ever seen you cry. If the petals are going to upset you that much I'll clear them up again. Please, please don't cry. I'm trying really hard to please you but if I'm still getting it wrong then just tell me and I'll fix it.'

The ache in Fia's chest increased. 'I appreciate it, honestly, but you don't have to try this hard. It's horribly, horribly humiliating when I know that we're heading for divorce.'

He paled. 'A divorce? No! I will *not* agree to a divorce, but I'll agree to anything else you want. I know you don't love me, but that doesn't mean we can't be happy.'

'It isn't me who wants a divorce, it's you! And I do love you, that's the problem.' The words broke from her like waves onto a rock, eroding the barriers she'd built between them. 'In a way I've always loved you. Part of me fell in love with you when I watched you teach your sister to swim. You were so patient with her. I had fantasies that Roberto would do that for me but all he ever did was hold me under the water. I loved you when you let me use the boathouse for a bolt-hole and didn't tell anyone. I loved you that night when you touched my shoulder because you knew I was upset and I still loved you when we made love.' The sobs made her almost incoherent. 'And I loved you when I married you. I have always loved you.'

For a moment there was no sound but his uneven breathing and the soft lap of the water against the wood of the boathouse.

'You love me? But…I forced you to marry me.' His voice was hoarse. Stunned and decidedly uncertain. 'I bullied you.'

'And that was when I loved you most of all,' she hiccuped. 'My mother gave birth to me but apparently that wasn't enough of a bond to stop her from leaving me. You didn't even *know* Luca but you knew he was your son and that was enough for you. You were willing to do anything for him simply because he was family. You have *no idea* how much I wish my parents had shown me even a fraction of that commitment. For your child's sake you were even prepared to marry a woman you didn't love, not just any woman but a Baracchi. And you were prepared to do anything to make it work.'

'Forget that—' his hands gripped her arms '—is it true that you love me? You're not just saying that for Luca's sake?'

'I wish I were, because then this would be easy instead of really, really hard.'

'Why is it hard?'

'Because it's so hard to love someone who doesn't love you back.'

He cursed softly and cupped her face in his hands. 'You think I don't love you? What do you think the past few weeks have been about? I've been falling over myself to please you.'

'I know. You were working really hard at it and that was actually quite crushing.'

'*Cristo*, you are making no sense at all.' He made an impatient sound and gave her a little shake. '*How* is it crushing that I worked hard to please you?'

'Because it didn't come naturally. You were doing it for Luca.'

His hands fell to his sides. He stared at her.

'Clearly we have misunderstood each other badly.'

'We have?'

'I had no idea you loved me. And you clearly have no idea how much I love you.'

Fia stared at him and her heart rate doubled. Hope bloomed as he slid his hands into her hair and took her mouth in a slow, erotic kiss. She wanted to ask him if she'd heard him correctly but it had been so long since he'd kissed her like this, she didn't want him to stop.

He lifted his mouth from hers with obvious reluctance. 'How could you ever *think* I'd want a divorce?'

'We stopped having sex.'

'I was so conscious that I'd forced you into this marriage and then you made those comments about me being insatiable—'

'I liked you being insatiable,' she muttered. 'When you stopped I assumed it was because you were bored with me, so I chose an especially sexy dress last night and you didn't even look at me.'

'And why do you think that was? In most things I am a very disciplined man but I've discovered that I have virtually no self-discipline where you are concerned.' His tone was raw. 'I'd promised myself that I wasn't going to make the first move. That I was going to let you come to me. You didn't.'

'I thought you didn't want me.'

He groaned and gathered her against him. 'We have both been blind and stupid. And we are going to start again from now.'

Fia closed her eyes for a moment, the feeling of relief so enormous that she couldn't speak. 'Do you really love me? This isn't to do with Luca?'

'This has nothing to do with Luca.' He murmured the words against her mouth. 'This has to do with you and me but I've made a total mess of things because now I can't make you believe me. Because I rushed you into this, you think it's all because of Luca. I love you, Fia. And if there were no Luca I would still love you.'

'If there were no Luca, we wouldn't have met again.'

'Yes, we would.' Lifting his hand, he stroked a finger over her jaw. 'I didn't even know about Luca when I came back. The chemistry between us is so powerful we would have ended up together sooner or later, you know we would.' He reached past her, picked up the box that had pride of place in the centre of the table. With a few flicks of his fingers he dispensed with the packaging and flicked it open.

Fia gasped. 'What's that?'

'It's an engagement ring. I'm proposing.'

She felt dizzy as she saw the size of the diamond. 'You already proposed, Santo. We're married. I have the ring.'

'You have a wedding ring. And, as I recall, I ordered you to marry me. Now I'm asking you to stay married to me. Always. Whatever life sends, good or bad, I want you by my side.' He breathed deeply, his eyes wary. 'Tell me honestly—would you *want* me to let you go?'

Warmth rushed through her, erasing all her doubts.

'Never. The fact that I know how committed you are to family is what makes me feel so secure,' she admitted. 'I know that no matter what happens we'll work it through.'

'*Ti amo tantissimo*, I love you so much,' he breathed, 'and

I'm sorry I've messed this up so badly.' He slipped the ring onto her finger, above the gold band he'd given her on their wedding day. It fitted perfectly.

Fia stared at the huge diamond, dazzled. 'I'll have to have twenty-four-hour security if I wear that.'

'Given that I don't intend to leave your side, that won't be a problem. I'll be your personal security.'

Overwhelmed, Fia flung her arms around him. 'I can't believe you love me.'

'Why? You are the strongest, most generous woman I've ever met. I cannot even bear to think about how it must have been for you to discover you were pregnant at a time when your whole world was collapsing. If I could put the clock back, I would, and I would never have left your side.'

'You did the right thing,' she said softly, sneaking another look at her ring. 'If you had come back that night it would simply have added more distress for my grandfather. You were being sensitive, and it was the right decision.'

'But it meant that you coped alone. Knowing what I do about you, I do not blame you for not telling me about Luca. I understand why you made the decision you did. Your childhood experience was so different to mine. And yet, even with that background you didn't repeat the pattern.' He slid his fingers gently through her hair. 'When you told me that you'd forbidden your grandfather to say a bad word about a Ferrara, I couldn't believe it.'

'Although he was shocked when he discovered I was pregnant, I think it actually gave him something to live for.'

'You married me believing that I didn't love you. That must have been incredibly hard.' He eased her away from him and she blushed.

'OK. Maybe it was a little. Do you know what's weird? I've always wanted to be a Ferrara. All my life, I wished I was in your family.'

'And now you are.' His hands cupped her face and his eyes gleamed with purpose. 'And once you're in the family, you're in it for ever.'

Smiling, she wrapped her arms around his neck. 'Once a Ferrara wife…'

'…always a Ferrara wife,' and he lowered his head to kiss her.

* * * * *

CLASSIC

Harlequin *Presents*

COMING NEXT MONTH from Harlequin Presents®
AVAILABLE JUNE 26, 2012

#3071 HEART OF A DESERT WARRIOR
Lucy Monroe
Sheikh Asad needs to secure his legacy, and Iris is the key.
Can she resist so determined a seduction?

#3072 SANTINA'S SCANDALOUS PRINCESS
The Santina Crown
Kate Hewitt
Pampered princess Natalia has swapped couture and
cocktails for photocopying! How long will she last working
for the devilishly handsome Ben Jackson?

#3073 DEFYING DRAKON
The Lyonedes Legacy
Carole Mortimer
Drakon Lyonedes has power, wealth, sex appeal...and any
woman he wants! Until beautiful Gemini Bartholomew enters
his life, that is...

#3074 CAPTIVE BUT FORBIDDEN
Lynn Raye Harris
Bodyguard Rajesh Vala must protect Veronica—whatever the
cost.... But Veronica has always rebelled against commands
and isn't making Raj's job easy!

#3075 HIS MAJESTY'S MISTAKE
A Royal Scandal
Jane Porter
Princess Emmeline is everything this desert king shouldn't
want... Posing as her twin sister and Makin's secretary, she's
playing with fire!

#3076 THE DARK SIDE OF DESIRE
Julia James
Business legend Leon Marantz exudes a dark power that
sends shivers through Flavia Lassiter's body—threatening to
shatter the icy shell protecting her heart.

You can find more information on upcoming Harlequin®
titles, free excerpts and more at www.Harlequin.com.

HPCNM0612

REQUEST YOUR FREE BOOKS!

Harlequin *Presents*

PASSION GUARANTEED SEDUCTION

2 FREE NOVELS PLUS
2 FREE GIFTS!

YES! Please send me 2 FREE Harlequin Presents® novels and my 2 FREE gifts (gifts are worth about $10). After receiving them, if I don't wish to receive any more books, I can return the shipping statement marked "cancel." If I don't cancel, I will receive 6 brand-new novels every month and be billed just $4.30 per book in the U.S. or $4.99 per book in Canada. That's a saving of at least 14% off the cover price! It's quite a bargain! Shipping and handling is just 50¢ per book in the U.S. and 75¢ per book in Canada.* I understand that accepting the 2 free books and gifts places me under no obligation to buy anything. I can always return a shipment and cancel at any time. Even if I never buy another book, the two free books and gifts are mine to keep forever.

106/306 HDN FERQ

Name _____ (PLEASE PRINT)

Address _____ Apt. #

City _____ State/Prov. _____ Zip/Postal Code

Signature (if under 18, a parent or guardian must sign)

Mail to the **Reader Service:**
IN U.S.A.: P.O. Box 1867, Buffalo, NY 14240-1867
IN CANADA: P.O. Box 609, Fort Erie, Ontario L2A 5X3

Not valid for current subscribers to Harlequin Presents books.

**Are you a current subscriber to Harlequin Presents books
and want to receive the larger-print edition?
Call 1-800-873-8635 or visit www.ReaderService.com.**

* Terms and prices subject to change without notice. Prices do not include applicable taxes. Sales tax applicable in N.Y. Canadian residents will be charged applicable taxes. Offer not valid in Quebec. This offer is limited to one order per household. All orders subject to credit approval. Credit or debit balances in a customer's account(s) may be offset by any other outstanding balance owed by or to the customer. Please allow 4 to 6 weeks for delivery. Offer available while quantities last.

Your Privacy—The Reader Service is committed to protecting your privacy. Our Privacy Policy is available online at www.ReaderService.com or upon request from the Reader Service.

We make a portion of our mailing list available to reputable third parties that offer products we believe may interest you. If you prefer that we not exchange your name with third parties, or if you wish to clarify or modify your communication preferences, please visit us at www.ReaderService.com/consumerschoice or write to us at Reader Service Preference Service, P.O. Box 9062, Buffalo, NY 14269. Include your complete name and address.

*Patricia Thayer welcomes you to Larkville, Texas,
in THE COWBOY COMES HOME—book 1 in the exciting
new 8-book miniseries, THE LARKVILLE LEGACY,
from Harlequin® Romance.*

REACHING THE BANK, Jess climbed down, smiling as she walked her mount to the water. "Wow, I haven't ridden like that in years."

"You're good."

"I'm Clay Calhoun's daughter. I'm supposed to be a good rider."

"You miss him."

She walked with him through the stiff winter grass to the tree. "It's hard to imagine the Double Bar C going on without him. He loved this land." She glanced around the landscape. "Now my brother runs the operation, but he'll be gone awhile." She released a breath. "I have to say we miss his leadership."

He frowned. "Is there anything I can do?"

"Thank you. You're handling Storm—that's a big enough help. It's just that it would be nice to have my brothers and sister here." She looked at him. "Do you have any siblings?"

He shook his head. "None that I know of."

"What about your father?" she asked.

He shook his head. "Never been in my life. I tried for years to track him down, but I never could catch up with him."

He caught the sadness etched on her face. "Johnny, I'm sorry."

He hated pity, especially from her. "Why? You had nothing to do with it. Jake Jameson didn't want to be found, or meet his son." He shrugged. "You can't miss what you've never had. I'm not much of a homebody, either. I guess that's why I like to keep moving."

Jess looked out over the land. "I guess that's where we're different. I've never really moved away from Larkville."

"Why should you want to leave? You have your business here and your home."

She smiled. "I had to fight Dad to live on my own. But I've got a little Calhoun stubbornness, too."

"You got all the beauty."

Johnny came closer, removed her hat and studied her face. "Your eyes are incredible. And your mouth… I could kiss you for hours."

She sucked in a breath and raised her gaze to his. "Johnny… We weren't going to start this."

"Don't look now, darlin', but it's already started."

Find out what happens between Johnny and Jess in
THE COWBOY COMES HOME by Patricia Thayer,
available July 2012!

And find out how Jess's family will be transformed
in the 8-book series:
THE LARKVILLE LEGACY
A secret letter…two families changed forever

This summer, celebrate everything Western
with Harlequin® Books!

www.Harlequin.com/Western

Harlequin Romance

THE LARKVILLE LEGACY

A secret letter…two families changed forever

Welcome to Larkville, Texas, where the Calhoun family has been ranching for generations. When Jess Calhoun discovers a secret, unopened letter written to her late father, she learns that there is a whole other branch of her family. Find out what happens when the two sides meet….

A new Larkville Legacy story is available every month beginning July 2012.

Collect all 8 tales!

The Cowboy Comes Home by **Patricia Thayer** *(July)*

Slow Dance with the Sheriff by **Nikki Logan** *(August)*

Taming the Brooding Cattleman by **Marion Lennox** *(September)*

The Rancher's Unexpected Family by **Myrna Mackenzie** *(October)*

His Larkville Cinderella by **Melissa McClone** *(November)*

The Secret that Changed Everything by **Lucy Gordon** *(December)*

The Soldier's Sweetheart by **Soraya Lane** *(January 2013)*

The Billionaire's Baby SOS by **Susan Meier** *(February 2013)*